three seven eleven

CW00850785

Chris and Bernard Ashley

three seven eleven

based on the Granada Television series
of the same name, also written by Chris
and Bernard Ashley

PUFFIN BOOKS

PUFFIN BOOKS

Published by the Penguin Group
Penguin Books Ltd, 27 Wrights Lane, London w8 5tz, England
Penguin Books USA Inc., 375 Hudson Street, New York, New York 10014, USA
Penguin Books Australia Ltd, Ringwood, Victoria, Australia
Penguin Books Canada Ltd, 10 Alcorn Avenue, Toronto, Ontario, Canada m4v 3b.
Penguin Books (NZ) Ltd, 182–190 Wairau Road, Auckland 10, New Zealand

Penguin Books Ltd, Registered Offices: Harmondsworth, Middlesex, England

First published 1993
10 9 8 7 6 5 4 3 2 1

Typeset by Datix International Limited, Bungay, Suffolk
Set in 12/14 pt Monophoto Bembo
Printed in England by Clays Ltd, St Ives plc

CHAPTER ONE

Kenny Bayfield lay in the cold grass, his nose to the soil and his eyes as unblinking as a seal's. He heard the shouts of the others playing football behind him and the words of the song his pal Jordan was rapping under his breath: but it was what was in front of him that had him held – the dust and the noise of the new school going up. The end of half term and then a week of extra holiday on top of that, and now the builders' fence was being knocked out to show the front of the school he and Jordan were going to have to go to – with some of those kids who'd just kicked them off their football pitch. He looked round at Jordan, who was one of those people who could sing all day as if he had a Walkman on, with never anything known coming out.

'Been in there yet?'

Jordan nodded, moaned to the end of a mystery verse. 'Who hasn't, pal? Every crack an' corner.'

Well, Kenny hadn't. Coming to a new school scared him rigid, without risking trouble with caretakers and builders.

'Like some little clinic or something. Hard carpets an' them midget chairs. Don't seem like a school . . .'

And he was right, it didn't: at least, not from the outside. The school Kenny had come from in Pennington had been one of those tall buildings with walls as thick as a castle; the school his dad had gone to, and his gran and grandad before. That had been a school where titches like Kenny got thumped and cat-called; but where at least the teachers knew him and what had happened to his mum; he knew who to run from and where to hide. But this move to Barton Wood had knocked him off balance more than anyone knew, and he had to have his Calpol at night to stop some of the pain in his stomach.

And Jordan knew, he was a smart old dude from a long while back. 'Stop frettin', Ken. Might not open Monday at all. Not with all this pandemonium still here. You got to think pos-it-ive!' He picked up his ball and disentangled his bike from Kenny's. 'Like me!' And after a quick high-five clap of their hands he went off across the goal-mouth just to annoy the others. Jordan Jenkins, proud of himself where Kenny was always the opposite.

Kenny looked back to the building site. Barton Wood Primary School, a long red brick bungalow with yellow painted triangles like some kit out of Early Learning. A new school and new teachers and new kids. He sank back into the grass. Cold February, cold field, cold soil: and he thought for a moment about his mother before he forced himself to stand up and be seen by anyone who might want to call him names.

'You little tyke!'

Mrs Pudsey swiped at Miranda with the *Sun* as the table the girl had turned over sent milk and cornflakes into her slippers and across the floor. Jumping back from the chaos she hit out wildly and kicked into the cat tray, swimming its muck into the swamp.

Miranda got to the door and was through it before her mother could get hold of anything lethal to throw. A plastic mug came after the girl like a missile.

'You seen what you've done? Come back here!'

But Miranda wasn't going to stop and go back to be battered. She kept on running, swung the front door open hard enough to pit the wall and went for the front path, her face twisted tight with what was hurting her inside. She jumped the tarpaulin which had blown off their scrap lorry and she ran out of the double gate.

Her mother came after, a strong woman with an outdoor face. 'Come here! Wait till I get my hands on you!' Never mind the milk down her shell suit, never mind any neighbours, she had an open grip on her which had to be filled with that kid's neck.

Miranda ran into the road, the shortest route away from getting grabbed: and when she saw the Peugeot 205 coming she was skinned as tight for time as a bullfighter. There was a tearing of rubber on the road, a loud horn and a shout from the driver as the girl half vaulted across the front of the bonnet and made off along the row of new houses on the other side.

Mrs Pudsey stopped at her gate. 'Just you wait!' That was her mouth. Her eyes told more: they showed no concern that the kid had nearly got run over. She just swore, and dropped her fist and turned back up the path and into the house, rocking the road with the slam she gave to the door.

The driver of the 205 sat back and swore quietly to herself. Already the perspiration had given her face a sheen, and she dabbed at that with the arm of her suit. She tidied her auburn hair in the mirror, found a tissue in the glove compartment, picked up the map of the area from the floor. A woman in her early thirties, she could have been an estate agent looking for a rendezvous; or, by the way she studied the map and seemed to be taking her bearings, someone who was getting to know the area for some reason of her own.

At the front of the new school, in what was left of the builders' compound, the architect was talking drains with the foreman, who still had an eye for the local yobs on the other side of the fence; they could ruin a morning's work with a football on a wet concrete path. The drainage run was blocked.

''Struth, that's chucking up in there!' Patrick Dunphy, the new caretaker, came out of the front of the school; he held his nose and jangled his keys.

4

Neither of the others looked up. 'You know we're opening Monday, got to have our lavvies working.' He said it with the wisdom of Einstein.

'You'll have to send out word not to eat too much breakfast!'

Dunphy nodded, as if he might actually put a blackboard at the gate. He was a young man, with his first solo school, and already this was his little kingdom and he was the main man, announced on his T-shirt. *The buck stops here.*

They were nodding to each other that it was very likely to be the disabled toilet causing the problem, but not so much as a blink in Dunphy's direction.

'Hold-ups, kiddies waiting to start school, now blocked lavvies — what the heck's going to hit us next?'

It was a football — and never mind *us*, it was him. It skimmed the top of the compound fencing in a dipping crack of a shot which would have done justice to Gazza. It caught Dunphy on the side of the head, slapped and stung. 'What the deuce . . .!' It spun him round to face the fence.

Over on the other side the arguments were starting about whether the shot had gone inside the coats or not, goal or goal-post: but a boy of about eleven was kicking up their side of the fence to look for the ball. 'Sorry, mate!' But his hard little face took the worth out of his apology. 'Over here!' He held up a hand for the ball to be returned.

'You little toe-rags!' It hadn't really hurt Dunphy,

but it had surprised him – enough to make him want to keep the ball till Monday – except the foreman had already kicked it back.

'That's the last time!' the foreman shouted. 'Once more an' I'm having it!' Which didn't please Dunphy either, because *he* was the caretaker, *he* kept balls when there were balls to be kept. It did underline the score though. The school hadn't been handed over yet. It wouldn't be the Irwell Valley Education Authority's responsibility until after the site meeting that afternoon.

Abusive shouts followed like shots looping over the fence – once the ball had gone back. The architect put a final cross on the disabled toilet with a Pentel and started to roll the plan. 'I've been designing schools for twenty years,' he said, 'and I still can't stand the sight of kids.'

'And there are teachers like that.' The foreman rubbed a memory off his backside.

Irwell Valley Education Authority
Barton Wood Primary School
Headteacher: Chris Sherry

Patrick Dunphy looked at the same sign with secret pride: shining scarlet paint which also gave his home telephone number at the bottom. He went back into the school to find his own small room and sit in it for just a few minutes before his lunch. His place: his own little office at Barton Wood Primary: it just needed a phone and his own computer.

Still outside, the architect stood looking at the school sign while the footballers shouted the odds over the fence. 'Headteacher: Chris Sherry,' he read. 'Well, the best of luck to him!' While Lee and Nicky and Jimmy and Sandra and a handful of others who were local to Barton Wood were wanting the ball at their feet, or on their heads, or long or short or near post or back door, any way which gave their silky skills a chance.

'Oh, yes! Who is this lad?' as Lee met a ball with the back of his neck and it bounced past Sandra, diving between the coats.

Kenny Bayfield watched them from behind the goal. He badly wanted in with them, but the only one he really knew – Sandra Smith from the other school – didn't carry enough clout to get him and Jordan into the game. And Jordan had gone now, anyway, so it was a slow walk pushing his bike across the field to the gate, and to Gran at home and whatever she'd spent the morning cooking him for his dinner.

'Hey up, little Kenny!' Sandra shouted. 'Should've helped me, I've let in seventeen!'

Chance would have been a fine thing! But even as she spoke another goal went past her and Kenny went to get it while she picked herself up from the mud.

'Ey! Sandra! You playin' or not?'

Kenny knew the kid's name, they were shouting it at him all the time like he was some star. Lee Rayner. And definitely the sort to always get what

7

he wanted: big for his age and looking hard enough to make you go out of your way not to bump into him by accident. You never saw him unless he was shouting the odds or giving someone one of those looks which made you pray to God to be his best mate, or something. One thing was dead sure. He'd be a rotten enemy to have.

Kenny got to the ball, and because he was so nervous all of a sudden he made a poor job of picking it up. He kicked the ball further on by mistake as he stooped, and then he dropped it as he went to grab it.

''Urry up, Midget! Come on, over 'ere!'

Kenny grabbed hold of the ball and he gave it a good boot to get it back: *Midget* was bad enough, he wasn't wanting *Wimp* to go with it. But he'd overdone it, and the ball when he kicked it went over Lee and over big Jimmy and over the others – and it went on over the builders' fence and into the school grounds again.

'You stupid dilk!'

The rest were disappointed, too, in bright scarlet words.

'Sorry!' Kenny shouted, trying to make up his mind which way to run.

'You will be!' Lee was over to him and throwing him down with force to dent the ground. He bent over him, angry red face, spat words, Kenny lying there like their little dog Montgomery showing submission to a pit bull. 'Get that back, Midget – or you see what you get!'

'Yeah. Course. Was going to, wasn't I?' Kenny wriggled away, got up and ran to the official gate of the school: well, he wasn't going to wind them up by climbing on their fence. But as he ran inside the compound the foreman already had the ball tucked under his arm and was making for the school's front door.

'I told you, didn't I? You can get this off the teachers, Monday!'

Kenny ran up to him: special pleading. 'Come on, pal, it wasn't them, it was me done that. Please! They're gonna batter me!'

'Be doing me a favour, then, won't they? An' I've clocked your face, son!' The foreman went inside: and Kenny knew this wasn't show. He'd lost them their ball till Monday, no doubt. He turned back to the gate – which was all strung across with the gang, all of them, except for Sandra. There was no running for it through them, there was no soft spot in that wall: and going back and doing the fence would only have them waiting for him over the other side.

'I never done it for the purpose. I just hit it too hard.'

'What I'm gonna do to you!' Lee came at him; and Kenny only stood his ground because there were builders about who wouldn't actually see him killed. 'I want that back, you hear, an' I ain't waiting till Monday. You get that back, son, or you're dead! D, A, E, D!'

'Stupid little dilk titch!' Nicky put his oar in,

too, another hard-looking case who would no doubt sit next to Kenny on Monday. Up to now it was only words, but it did look like staying that way. If they were going to hit him they'd have come at him right off.

'I'm having me sav an' chips,' Lee told Kenny, 'an' if that ball ain't back after, I'm comin' to get you, Midget!' And he led the rest away, with backward looks of no hope slung over their shoulders.

Kenny looked around, looked over at the new pub next door to the school: and it suddenly gave him just the smallest measure of hope. Just the smallest. The pub would be where the builders went for their lunch; so perhaps afterwards they'd be a bit more friendly. Well, he could hope. He turned back to look in through the white smeared glass of the door of the school. In the corridor the man with the ball was talking to the caretaker, giving it to him. Kenny opened the door a crack, suddenly decided to look pathetic for them, to chance his arm after all. But they didn't see him, they were talking computers or something, looking at stuff the caretaker had got in his bag. No, the time wasn't right: the time never was, when you were in the muck.

He stared down at the hardened mud of the builders' compound, where the rose bushes or whatever would go. It didn't matter how you tried to soften up the look of a school, it was always hard inside, it was always aggravation for a kid like him.

He breathed in deeply and let it out in a long, thin scare of a sigh. And it was no good forever telling someone, not as many times as he would have to: people got fed up with a whining little face. No, you just had to soldier on. Which was what he was going to have to do right now: get home to his gran and try to pretend he wasn't sick to the pits with Barton Wood.

CHAPTER TWO

Gran Bayfield climbed up the kitchen stool. The kitchen in their new house had been fitted out with a breakfast counter because the builders had impressed her with the up-to-date look of it: but no one had foreseen the height problem. How long it would be before the whole thing was ripped out and a table and chairs bought again was anybody's guess.

Kenny was already up there, pushing sausage and mash and peas into new places on his plate, no appetite. Gran's plate was up there steaming next to his, and she was coming up after.

'What a performance for getting a bite to eat!' She missed a rung and went at it again. 'Like going blessed mountaineering!' She made it up there and looked back across the kitchen at the cooker. 'But if I've forgotten anything we'll go without.' She looked at her plate, looked at Kenny. 'What's up with you?' She went for the funny bone. 'Eat up, you never know −' she prodded his sausage with her knife − 'they might've stuffed a fiver in there for luck!'

But Kenny wasn't up to being jollied, pushed his plate away. His gran shook her head. 'Been out of school too long, that's what your trouble is.' He stared at the good food going cold. Even if he could have got it past the great lump in his throat his foaming stomach would only have thrown it back.

'Delay here, hold up there – children need their education. But if they don't open Monday there'll be ructions, I can tell you!' Gran Bayfield shoved half a sausage in her mouth and went at it as if she were chewing up those responsible. 'Come on, Tin Ribs, there's a bit of ice cream for after ...' She put the plate back in front of him. But Kenny was close to tears, and she didn't push too hard.

If only she knew! Kenny thought. Why couldn't you tell people about the Lee Rayners of the world without sounding weak as water? A sudden light-headedness came over him and he had to grip the stool hard to stop himself coming off it. Why did there have to be Lees in the world at all?

'Go on, then, get down: but I'll want to see a decent dinner eaten when your dad's in.' She reached over and forked his sausage on to her own plate. Kenny cleared the rest into the pedal bin and went off out through the back door. 'Poor little cock!' she said, watching him go: before she realized she was alone in the kitchen on her high stool. 'Now how the heck do I get down from here?'

Kenny wasn't alone on the Barton Wood Estate

waiting for the new school to open on the Monday. There were others who had moved into the new houses going up with the school, and a few who were transferring from the overcrowded school on the other side of the canal. And there was just one whose parents had moved in to run the local shop, Vasisht's General Store.

Right now Kompel Vasisht was crouched on the canal bank trying to entice a tiddler to swim on to her palm. The spring sunshine was warm on her head, the air was clean and clear after Willesley, and she had only just failed to do this country thing and catch a tiddler. She smiled, rippled the water with a finger, said some soft name to the darting fish.

Plunk! Something hard and blackened landed on the water where the fish had been. It floated. Kompel looked up. On the opposite bank of the canal two kids sat hunched, take-aways in their hands and their eyes on her as they pushed food into their mouths. They'd come from nowhere, silent as snipers moving into place. She got up. Everything got spoiled: the whole world was a spoiled place.

Lee Rayner and Nicky Power were eating their saveloy and chips: Lee the leader, but Nicky known to be twice as hard.

'Reckon that's deep?' Loud enough to be heard across ten canals.

'One way to find out.'

'Chuck someone in! Do girls sink or do they float?' A voice smeared with sneer.

Kompel had forgotten fishing. She had got up and was edging along her side of the canal towards the bridge which would take her back towards the shop. But the pair on the other bank had got up too, and were eating and spitting along towards the same bridge she was heading for. It was always the same: you might think you were out for a walk but you usually ended up having to run. She got there first, muddied her track suit trousers in a scramble up the side, thought she might just have time to make it across and on to the estate before they could get near her, but – the bridge was taken. Someone else was there in front. Climbing up from underneath was another kid, white, blond, about her age and talking all sorts of rubbish.

'I'm a troll! Fol-de-rol!' He was smiling, looked as if he wasn't part of these others.

And she was right, because the others had heard him and were taking the rise, pushing each other at him as they came up on their side of the bridge. 'Oh, he's a troll!'

'Sausage roll!' Nicky Power threw the remains of his saveloy at the boy's head. 'You here an' all, Scud?'

The boy dodged to let the saveloy miss him, wasn't running anywhere. 'Came yesterday.' He turned his head to Kompel. 'They with you?'

'No way!'

'Wanna bit more?' Lee Rayner looked as if he wasn't sure whether to throw the end of his saveloy or eat it.

'Thought this was all gonna be new!' Nicky Power spat again, on to the ground on purpose, and not into the water. 'Same ol' snobs!'

Lee decided to throw, followed Nicky's saveloy with the remains of his own. 'Here y'are, boy! Up an' beg!' It also missed, so he followed it with the end of his chips, the lot going over the parapet and plopping into the water.

Nicky pushed him. 'You vandal, Rayner! It's people like you let the ozone layer down!'

Lee grabbed back, fierce. 'Yeah, an' it's people like me let your trousers down!' And with a push and a shove and a shout, all chewed chip and saveloy pickings, they chased each other like a couple of fighting dogs – their commotion looking like it was covering the fact that they hadn't known quite what to do with their aggro for Kompel and this other one.

Kompel was left looking at the boy: someone else just moved in and on his own. And tall, nice-looking in a posh sort of way. She wished she hadn't come straight out from the shop, would have liked to be in one of her more sparkly tops and trousers.

'You going to the new school?' he was asking her. 'Or are you too old?'

That pleased her, somehow. 'No. I mean yes. No!' Now she was tripping up like an idiot, sounding half the age she wanted. 'I'm not too old, and I am going to the new school.'

He actually looked quite pleased about that. 'Me as well.'

They stared at each other, questions ready but nothing personal getting pulled out for asking quite fast enough.

'You know them?' Kompel tossed her head at the rowdies, who were still jumping on each other's backs as they went off into the older streets on their side of the water.

'That first one to throw stuff, that's Nicky Power. He was at the other school. He has to do all that, reckons his dad's in Strangeways.'

'What for?'

'Having him, likely!'

She laughed. 'And is he in prison?'

The boy shrugged. 'I don't know. I don't go visiting.' He looked at Kompel, shoved his hands in the pockets of a newish leather top. 'Other one's just a pain. Where you from?'

'Willesley.' Kompel watched his face. Usually they meant which country. He was nodding, no follow-up questions. She leaned back on the parapet like someone relaxed, just a bit of a show: but the sun genuinely seemed to be warmer now. 'I was trying to catch a fish.'

'You'd have more luck trying to catch an old trolley in here . . .'

Right, she thought, and it was a sad and rotten fact of life. 'Thought this was going to be different. Where we come from it was all chuck it down and step over it.'

'Oh, head up, it's not that bad . . .'

'No?'

'Everyone likes to hear a good splash.'

Kompel laughed again. 'Hope that's it. Only it was a tip of a place, our bit of Willesley – we never had nothing like this, no open spaces near, no grass and water and fishes living . . .'

The boy turned back to look into the canal, which ran fast and dangerous in the middle where they were standing.

'But people are all the same, don't matter where . . .' Except that even as she said it Kompel was thinking how this boy looked as if that might not be true about him. He was a bit different, all right. She smiled at him, tried to think of something on the plus side to say, because she'd never thought of herself as a whiner – more of a winner, as it went.

But a car took her attention away, pulling up on her side of the bridge. A woman in a smart suit was getting out of a 205 and looking round about her, referring back to a map she had in her hand; which she suddenly threw on to the front seat and started coming across towards them.

'Do you know if there's a chemist's shop near here?' She had a hand to her head in the sort of headache mime people do; you saw all sorts of it in the shop: headaches, stomach aches, hands clutched at throats . . . Kompel didn't give the boy a chance to answer. She jumped in because she knew there wasn't.

'Not a chemist's. What is it you want?'

'Just something to sort a headache.'

Kompel pointed. 'Down there, Vasisht's General Store, first right and it's on the left.'

'Oh, lovely.' Some relief, and a nice smile. She had a kind face, with auburn hair and blue eyes: she could have been a doctor, except then she wouldn't have been wanting tablets.

'It's mine, my mum and dad's.' Kompel was telling it to the boy as well, whichever way her eyes were looking.

'Handy I asked, then!'

'We do aspirins, paracetamol, analgesics . . .'

'Very impressive. Plenty of choice.' The woman went back to her car. 'Thank you.'

'And homeopathic!'

The boy looked pleased for her. 'Think you made a sale.'

'Yeah.' She was suddenly dry in the mouth. 'Anyhow, got to go; got to help.'

'In the shop?'

'Day out over!' But she didn't move, not for a moment. She was thinking, they'd ended up with him knowing a lot more about her than she knew about him.

'See you Monday, then.'

'Yeah, all right, see you Monday.' Well, she'd find out.

'Or I might see you in your shop.'

'Yeah.' She'd look out for that. What she liked was, he smiled when most kids thought it was soft to have any look on their tight faces. 'What's your name?'

'David. David Kent.'

'Ah –' As if it were the answer to something she

really wasn't bothered about, as if she were only being polite: but as she walked off the bridge, going the way the 205 had gone, she knew very well that David Kent was staring after her, all the way, and she liked that. All thought of those two yobs went out of her head, because her high hopes for Barton Wood had just returned. She'd found a friend. And what difference did it make that he was a boy?

CHAPTER THREE

When Kenny went to the shed the hose had fallen off its hook and tangled itself through the spokes of his bike. Days were like that: and the more pulling you did to get yourself sorted the worse coils tightened. Mooching days, his grandad called them: leave things alone, shove your hands in your pockets and go off for a long mooch till tea-time, because you're going to solve nothing till the earth has had a good spin.

The cost of freeing the bike was having to stand all the gardening tools in new places. Well, he'd sort them later. The trouble was, there wasn't the time to give the earth a good spin: and going for a mooch was only going to bring him up against Lee Rayner somewhere. So he might as well face up to his devils and go to try his luck round at the new school. They'd have had their pub lunch by now: they just might give him a burp and a pardon.

He came round through the side gate and bumped on his bike down on to the unmade road. Drainage covers stood up like stepping stones, and a furniture van was following a tacking course as if mines had been sown. He didn't have time to hang about, he wanted this sorted so he could sleep tonight. Getting up speed, Kenny cycled round the van and set his head down for the school. He hated anything hanging over him, especially a kicking-in.

'Oi!'

But the rotten day it was, Lee Rayner was there like bad news, he'd come out from the other side of the van and was grabbing at Kenny's handlebars. His face was pushed close, all saveloys and onion sauce.

'You got my ball, Midget?'

'Gi's a chance. Just had my dinner.' Or Gran and the dog had. 'Just goin' to get it.'

'I wasn't giving my gob a go, son, I want that ball back today! That's a casey!'

OK, Kenny knew that. He knew you couldn't let a casey get lost the way you could a plastic.

'My dad give me that!' And it was said as if the kid were talking crown jewels. He jerked a twist on Kenny's handlebars, put him well out of true. 'I'll scuddin' have you if you don't! You'll wake up stone dead, pal!'

Lee Rayner backed off and kicked his way up the road, singing a violent song. And Kenny, not for the first time since his mother had died, was left trying to sort the twist, and thinking of the relief it would bring to be stone dead.

When he got to the school, trying to keep a straight line while his handlebars went off at an angle, the builders' fence was coming down and being loaded on to a lorry. From the road the school was suddenly starting to look like a school, the place wasn't being built any more, it was finished, nearly ready, waiting for him and all the rest to come on Monday.

If he wasn't in the General Hospital . . . He took a good hard look at the workmen: and it was obvious from the off that his soft idea of a plan wasn't any way going to work. Everyone was shouting at everyone else for things to be cleared out of the road while the fence was shifted, and no one looked a penn'orth kinder for having had a pint or two in the pub. The foreman, the one Kenny would have gone for, was giving someone a rucking for splitting a sack of cement, so there wouldn't be any point going up and asking him: and the young ones with the tattoos were having a Friday afternoon swear-up over their pay packets, so they weren't favourite for asking, either.

He'd have left it if he could: but the hard twist Lee had put on his handlebars was only going to remind him all weekend how strong the kid was — which did jack him up to try to do something. And as if someone were smiling down at him, at just that moment a sudden chance opened up and took him in through the gates as if he'd shouted 'Abracadabra'. The main doors of the school were held back by fire extinguishers while the sanding equipment was coming out, and right then, as he was looking, a plywood sheet of fencing was being carried across the front of the school like some large piece of stage scenery. It gave Kenny the in he needed. With the plywood carried by two men whose heads were round one side of it, he ran behind it on the other and was in through the school door almost before he'd thought what he was doing.

He stood with his back to a new wall, looked around. Old Jordan had been right, it was a neat little school: smart, all brick and shiny tiles and doors with a high gloss of hard paint on them. The signs were up — 'Secretary', 'Headteacher', and so on — and direction arrows flew this way and that at easy levels to read. Furniture was stacked up high in plastic wraps, and there was the smell of new dust finding good places to settle. Never mind the casey, Kenny's stomach squeezed at the Monday morning to come and a pang of toilet pain had a quick hold of him: but he got rid by starting to run around and look in all the likely places. In corners, behind doors, on bookshelves, in cupboards, he scooted about with his eyes on the scan like a tracker dog. No sweat, back at his old school he'd have known where they'd have put a confiscated ball — the caretaker in his boiler house, the staff on the cleaners' cupboard — but here, it could be anywhere. All right, he had a bit of freedom, he was lucky the builders were all outside, but where the heck was the ball? He hadn't got for ever. He ran to a corridor window and looked out on to Monday's playground. Had they got it out there with them, had a game with it at dinner time? A dumper truck was moving off, and someone was sweeping the sand off the tarmac: he could see where he'd be lining up: but there wasn't any sight of a ball. And, worse, with the outer fence completely down, who could he see standing there staring at the school? Lee Rayner and his football gang looking like a hit squad, hands in their pockets and that twisted just-you-wait! look on their faces.

He didn't know if he'd been spotted; but there was no going out just yet, no way, not without the ball. So what had he got to lose by going on looking for it? Only the getting caught, and having a policeman round to the house for trespass, and being blamed for the break-ins and broken windows! Well, he was in for it anyway, wasn't he? Hell! Kenny could see how people ended up murdering.

He came away from the window: and, as he turned, the next thing he saw was a tall new cupboard in dark veneer, and on the top of it, crammed against the low ceiling, was Lee Rayner's casey. It couldn't be seen from beneath, you had to be a bit away to see where that cocky foreman had stuck it: but there it was. Pure sorted! Kenny had a quick think, would save his dancing for joy for later. It was a ladder or a table job to get it down, he reckoned. There was no way anyone could jump up and get that back, not even a kid of normal height. But the good news was, there were tables and chairs stacked for the shifting, any number, make any height you wanted. It was only a question of people keeping out of the way while he set to and did it. And the ideal table was handy, one of the new ones, already off the stack and being used for mugs of tea and an old kettle. Great, that could be slid across a treat; and about the right height if he put a chair on top of it. He took a last quick look about him. And still there was no one around, all the work was going on outside with their great clear-up. He couldn't believe his luck.

Right! Half a minute, Kenny reckoned. Table dragged, chair thrown up, ball grabbed; a quick jump down – leave everything, good luck to the lot of them – and out through the door and let anyone see him who cared. He'd get through any grabbing hands like a wing-forward with a good wind behind him: because if there was one plus to being small it was a pair of quick feet and being a dodger. One more very last quick look round: only him and the dust: so it was now, it was go!

He went for it. But even as Kenny grabbed for the table a car drew up by the front entrance, a door slammed, and the sounds of men's voices came in ahead. The headteacher, an inspector, the caretaker – any one could mean trouble for him. What sort of a start would he have on Monday if he was found skulking in here today?

He left the table, the milk rocking in its cracked jug and his heart in a skid, and he scuttled deeper into the building – through the first doors and into the school hall. Oh, Mum, he was right in it now!

There was no way out he knew of, and if these people came on in he was going to be caught like some rotten little crook. He saw the look on his gran's face, the shake of his grandad's head, the telling off his dad would give him, who'd remind him how much sadness he'd got on his plate already. And he stood waiting there because there was absolutely nothing else he could do. His way out was through that front door – and still not without that casey if he could help it.

A man called Gerry Alderwood was blocking it, however. Not that Kenny would know, but Alderwood represented the County Planners, the people who had agreed to the school being built and who had overseen it. Gerry Alderwood made important decisions all day, he passed or failed people's projects, imposed penalties like some visiting magistrate and, full of his own importance, was the sort who wore a site safety hat with a mohair suit and trod over builders' rubble in shoes by Pierre Cardin. In his late thirties, he was about the age of Kenny's dad, but with a height and a confidence and a falling lock of hair that Kenny's dad would have given his teeth for.

'Afternoon.' He was into the building now and being met by the foreman.

'Afternoon, Gerry.' But it sounded more uptight than pally.

Through his crack in the door Kenny saw others following: a labourer carrying plans, and the man in the sheepskin who had been about outside when the ball was taken that morning. And they were coming this way, towards the hall. They had 'Important Meeting' written all over them.

Kenny got across that school hall in a speed he'd never manage in a PE lesson; he got across it and through the door at the other side to one of the classroom areas, stopped the thing swinging while he caught his breath, and he waited there, one eye on low cupboards where he might stretch out and get missed, the other on windows and doors to the outside.

Back on the other side of the hall doors Gerry Alderwood was taking a dictating machine from his inside pocket, looking at the buttons on it as if the thing were new. He clicked one of them and started talking into it. 'Site meeting to hand over Barton Wood School, from builders to Education Authority.' He clicked it off. 'Make a start, shall we?' Not that he was giving them any option; that wasn't Gerry Alderwood's way. Click. 'Those present – Alderwood, County Planning . . .' He held the machine to the others, in turn.

'Hamilton Smith, Architects.'

'Ted Edgeworth, the builders.' The foreman looked to the front door of the school, looked at his watch. 'Headteacher?' he asked.

'Not essential.' Alderwood was keen to get on. 'But we could have done with the girl from Finance with the penalty figures.' His mouth gave a little twitch of frustration: not that he was going to be held up. 'I've got a squash court booked for five.'

He led the way, pointing a silver biro at this radiator, at that course of bricks.

From behind the doorway on the other side of the hall Kenny couldn't hear the words but he could see those suits coming in. A tape-measure was out, and little notebooks: people tapping, running their hands over the walls; a good look being had all round – and they were going all over the school, he could tell. They were coming his way and every way. He pulled himself back. He hated being small, but it sometimes had its good side: like, he could hide in little places where people wouldn't dream of looking, and he could get in and out through cracks no wider than ventilation. Now he ran across a work bay to the nearest window and he put his strength to the handle. It wasn't meant to open far but it'd open far enough for him – except the thing was shut tight, too tight, like Rayner doing his handlebars. He ran to the next one: it was the same: and behind him those voices were getting louder all the while. In a panic now, he looked around him: where could he get himself hidden? He bet all the cupboards in here were locked.

Kenny heard the toot of another car. Outside, where the boy desperately wanted to be, the Peugeot 205 which had been seen round the streets had pulled up, and the woman with the headache had got out. And while Kenny dived for locked cupboard after locked cupboard she drew herself up and with just a quick look at the scarlet school sign she walked briskly into the building. She caught up with the others, who were talking toilets.

'Ah, good you're here.' Gerry Alderwood gave her more of a twitch than a nod. 'Make notes for Borough Treasurer, will you?' He waved his little recorder: 'I shall have my own.' Edgeworth and the architect were explaining how the floor of the disabled toilet had had to be dug up to free the blockage. 'And make a particular note of that in case there's a fight later on.' He waved his hand at the woman, which could almost have served as a practice stroke for five o'clock.

'What?' It really was as if the woman hadn't heard him properly.

Alderwood sighed: Finance really couldn't get the staff these days. 'I asked you to make a note . . .'

'And who are you to ask me to make notes?'

She was tall: no taller than he, but he suddenly seemed to be looking up at her, not down. 'Alderwood, Planning.' His tired voice was anticipating a dispute between departments.

'Sherry. Education.'

'Ah! Not Finance.' Another backhand, just as Patrick Dunphy came out of his room with a light jacket over his arm. 'Forget it, lovie,' Alderwood told the woman. 'We're talking drains and money, so if you want to be checking furniture or counting beads or something, please feel free.'

Ted Edgeworth was looking as if he were trying to interrupt in spite of having just swallowed a wasp: but the auburn-haired woman with the hard blue eyes and the smart suit was in no need of an ally.

'If you're talking toilets, I'm talking toilets, too.' She tapped her own lapel with a strong finger. 'Sherry. Mrs. Christine – or Chris. Headteacher. Representing the staff and children who will actually be using this school.' She nodded to Ted Edgeworth. 'Hello, Ted.'

'Ah.' Alderwood took it like a just word from an umpire. 'Oh dear, who's a patsy?'

'Dunphy. Patrick.' The caretaker stepped forward to be introduced.

But Mrs Sherry was only taking breath, a lift of the hand to Dunphy while Ted Edgeworth started counting bricks. 'I have kept out of your hair through all the delays –' she told the man from County Planning – 'by a great effort of patience. But I'm here now to take the place over on behalf of the staff and the children and to start running it from Monday next. So if we've got lavs that don't flush, I'm the one who needs to know!'

'And me,' Dunphy put in. 'I'm hot on lavvies!'

'Profuse apologies.' Alderwood checked that his recorder was off and moved it from right hand to left as he shook with the headteacher. 'Welcome aboard.'

At which Mrs Sherry pulled out a notebook of her own, ready to put the disabled toilet on her own hit list. There were no children with physical disabilities due to be enrolled; but no one was going to hang about getting the toilet fixed.

Everybody nodded.

Behind the hall door Kenny was trying the last cupboard in the work bay, and trying to do it without making a sound. No luck! Everything was locked except one of these – and that was stuffed tight with spare shelves for all the others. He turned full circle on himself twice: once this way, once that. There was nowhere he could hide: nowhere at all: and he couldn't just get behind something, these people were looking everywhere.

'I'll say cheerio, then, to one and all,' Dunphy was saying. 'I've been here since sparrows. If everything's all right?'

No one took any notice: and with a jangle of keys and a swish of his hold-all and a last look over his shoulder in case anyone was waving, the caretaker went.

Kenny was back at the hall door in the remote hope they'd been diverted into the lavatory and he could get a run at the front entrance of the school. But, no chance: there they all were, and there was the caretaker going. Which meant that all the back doors to the outside stood a good chance of being locked as tight as Strangeways. Something turned over inside him. He was mousetrapped in here something wicked, caught as in kipper – with only one possible thing he could do, get himself further into the building. But he hadn't wanted that, he wanted out, not in: he looked to where a curtain hung at an archway, leading through to another work area. That was deeper into a corner, tighter into the trap.

'Rubbish in the manholes, broken windows, gravel through the skylights!' The long-haired man in the sheepskin was talking to the tall woman, coming across the hall. 'Kids! Any children found on this site should be prosecuted for trespass, full extent of the law. Get them and their parents into court, put 'em away and make 'em pay.'

But there weren't any other options: Kenny had got to run wherever there was room: there was no way he was getting caught by that one! In his panic he nearly had a table over and he only just stopped a rack of technology tools from dismantling itself across the floor. Bent double like a soldier on the run he swung himself round one corner, round two, lost the voices for a bit, and ran into another bay which had to be the Nursery. It had to be: there was a cooker, a little house, a tricycle. But that wasn't what struck. What struck was the state of it. Chaos. World War Three. Everything was all over the place, prams and trikes on their sides, big building bricks in heaps of plastic rubble – and smeared across the facing wall in bright red paint was a big word 'hat', the letters still running down it like spilling blood. And sitting on the carpet with a pile of new dolls all undressed was a girl in a nurse's hat, a girl he'd seen around the streets and kept his distance from, Miranda Someone, whose mother was always out on the pavement shouting her name.

''Struth!' Kenny wasn't stopping, he ran on through. 'Get out, get off, get away!' he pushed at

33

the girl as she suddenly jumped up with a doll and started running with him. 'Clear off, I'm not taking the blame for that!' But as he tried to get himself free he heard the voices again and, feeling sick to the gut, he knew it was just his luck that he wasn't going to shake this one off in a hurry.

CHAPTER FOUR

Mrs Sherry's voice was sounding mild right now, but it still had that depth to it which made people pay attention. Even the architect was having to let her have her say as they came from the hall and through the first bay into the second.

'You shouldn't be so full of doom and gloom,' she told him, 'locking everyone up!' She waved an elegant hand around the part of her new school they'd come into. 'None of us can wait for Monday now. Youngsters aren't all as terrible as you think. They'll be delighted with a new place like this.' She smiled at him, and he gave a little bow: the school was all to his design, after all: there were new work surfaces, computer bays, low-level sinks and neat rows of hat and coat hooks under polished wooden shelves. 'Give children the best and they'll soon rise to your expectations.'

They had come to the Nursery, just turned the corner into it: and it took a second or so to sink in, as if for an instant they thought this could be a new way for a Nursery to be. Except he was the architect, and she was the headteacher.

'"Hat"?' he queried, looking at the wall: just something to say in the shock.

'"Hate"!' She could have been quietly correcting a reader.

'Ah!' Words were really hard to come by.

'A very destructive feeling.'

The others caught up with the two figures of stone standing there.

The room was a tip: looking at it, it was as if stuff was still flying about: there wasn't a thing in the room that hadn't been thrown out or turned over or taken apart. Ted Edgeworth swore, and didn't apologize for it.

'"Hate",' the architect told Alderwood, 'a very destructive feeling amongst perfectly normal youngsters.'

Mrs Sherry rounded on the contractors. 'How could this have happened?' She stooped to a doll.

'This paint's still wet.' Alderwood was touching the wall like forensic.

'And this doll's still warm.'

They all looked at one another. They had just come through an empty hall and two empty working areas. So, whoever had done this was ahead of them: the same thought seemed to strike them all at the same moment. As one, their breathing lightened, their feet went soft on the floor, and with the tread of a search party in an unsafe building they all advanced through the next curtained doorway into the back corridor.

At the rear of the school Kenny Bayfield was pulling at the playground door. It was locked solid. The girl stood watching him, head to one side, nursing a doll. He pushed her out of his way, tried another window, started his panicky turning round and round again.

'They're here!' he hissed. 'They're coming to get you and they're coming to get me! But don't you say I had anything to do with that mess!' He shook a fist at her; but he could just see it. He'd be up in court Monday morning charged with all this lot – and be the biggest let-down his family had ever had. They could do without this, all of them – his dad, his gran and grandad. Rayner's football not getting returned and the battering he'd get for that was nothing to what this lot would land him in. He swore, and he pushed the girl again: anything to get her apart from him: against a door, which moved a fraction further closed, then opened, just a crack. An open door leading into a small dark cupboard!

Into a small dark chance!

People were starting to shout to them to come out and give themselves up: come out, come out wherever they were. Well, some rotten serious game this was! He could hear their feet clumping and table legs skidding; a stack of chairs went over like an earthquake and the woman shouted, 'Careful!'

He thought no more about it. Last chance, only chance! Kenny squeezed himself into the cupboard and had no option but to let the girl in with him, else she'd only tell them where he was. She pulled the door tight in on them, turned the handle, and he could tell that the doorway was metal framed, a strong-room door, a door to a security cupboard. Eyes wide in the dark, he tried to see somewhere to hide: if he could get in here, so could the others. He could just see shelves going high, and a small skylight which gave a bit of a glim to the place, once his eyes got used, and then expensive computer stuff, and disc packs and cardboard boxes of blanks. Instantly, Kenny was up the shelves to try the skylight, but it was never meant to be opened. All the same, the top shelf was wide, and it was empty . . .

And already this Miranda was up there after him, doll and all.

'I'm not with you!' He tried to shrug her off. 'I never done all that!'

'Oh, they'll know, won't they?' she said, sarcastic, and forced him to make room with her elbow.

The cupboard door opened.

They froze like carcasses in a butcher's back room.

'Store cupboard,' someone said. The person came in, poked among the boxes on a lower shelf, went out and shut the door tight.

'Got a key to this?' they heard him say.

'Special one. Caretaker's gone off with the other.' And within seconds there was the double, triple twist of a key in a very solid lock, and muffled voices going on about the hooligans getting away through the front. And, too late now, Kenny realized the school went round in a square; if he'd kept on going he'd have got back to the front door and out. Let these others get into the hall and he could have climbed up for the ball and been off. He laid back on the shelf and he swore at the ceiling; Jordan and the rest who'd been all over the school, they would have known: the real intruders.

The woman was going on about her Nursery and having to open Monday: and voices started getting raised when someone else said they were done for the weekend, the Nursery would have to wait. But it wasn't the state of the Nursery that was suddenly gripping at Kenny in a panic. It was what they were saying actually meant. It hit him like something cold down the neck. They'd locked this solid door and now they were going off – for the weekend! This was Friday, and outside these people were talking Monday! He only had this one last chance to get out from this death trap. He struggled to sit up from where Miranda was holding him tight against the wall, but there was no room between the shelf and the ceiling. He'd slid in, he'd have to slide out. He wriggled and he pushed and he tried to punch. He was going to shout out, get rescued. Lee Rayner? A sad Dad? So what? What were they against a suffocated Kenny?

But the girl had got him at the throat. 'Don' be so soft! They'll have us up the Juvenile!'

Well, he didn't care. There was air up the

Juvenile, there were big rooms, windows, there was space up the Juvenile. And there was air and space in Borstals, and playing fields, and exercise yards. Held down, squeezed between her and a hard wall up on a top shelf with nowhere to lift his head, with an iron door shut tight on him and a window above with no opening, he opened his mouth to yell out and get caught.

'Shut it!' The doll had dropped to the floor and she was clamping his mouth with one hand, pinching his nose with the other. He fought, used knees, feet, but she'd got him tight and she was strong. She had her legs across the space and was pushing against the other wall so she had all the purchase. She had him tight and he couldn't breathe no matter how he humped and pumped.

He went limp, he gave in, like a beaten dog, again. She, slowly, very slowly, let go the grip on his nose so that he could breathe in the dusty cupboard air; she gradually unclamped his mouth. And he didn't move.

'Right. You do what Miranda tells you,' she said.

'But they're going!' He tried to make himself sound reasonable, a nice voice meant to get her to see some sense. 'They're going off till next Monday!'

But all she could do was laugh. 'So we got a weekend on our own!' She let go of him altogether and climbed down to pick up the doll, starting stroking it and muttering love in its ear. Above which he heard the rev of cars and the shut of a distant door.

'Help! Ey! Let me out!' Kenny was down off the shelf like someone falling off a top bunk. He banged at the door with his fists, kicked at it as hard as a police raid and shouted the top strain of his voice. 'Come back here! Let me out! Oi!' He turned to the girl, was seriously close to tears. 'No one'll know where I am!'

'No one'll care where I am!' She looked around. 'Let's see what stuff they got. We can have a muck about.' She started picking up cardboard boxes of new discs, tipped them on the floor, kicked them about.

'You're barmy!' Kenny made another mad assault on the door. 'Help! Let me out!' But no one was hearing him, and he knew it. The front door was locked and everyone was gone – except for this girl standing here with computer discs under her feet, a nurse's hat on her head and a doll in her arms being cuddled like real. He put his back to the door and stared at her.

And she stared back: full in the face while she opened her mouth wide and screamed, long and loud and violent: that same scream that had started her day.

Outside, nobody heard it. With the site deserted and the big match abandoned, the only sound was the rich crackling noise Gerry Alderwood's Mercedes made as it negotiated the sheen of sand and brick dust left on the new tarmac.

Ted Edgeworth watched it go. They always crackled like that, he reckoned, posh cars on a site: just like they made it sound on telly whenever old Inspector Morse drove off to solve a murder.

Ted turned the key to lock the school door, and, taking a couple of steps back, looked over at his own van. No chance of hearing anything above the racket that old banger made. He smiled, though, as he took in the front of the new school building. They might not drive great motors, but by heck Ted Edgeworth and his lads knew their business. He'd like to see an Inspector Morse or even a Gerry Alderwood build a school like this one.

He'd thrown the keys into the air and caught them with a proud snap before the smile drained away and the familiar foreman's tension returned to his stomach. He'd told them at dinner-time, hadn't he? 'Get that sign up!' And now look; the headmistress stopping her car and cleaning the cans off and trying to stand the thing up herself.

'We'll 'ave this up for you Monday morning, love.' Ted helped her rest the board against the wall and tried not to seem concerned as he retreated to the gates.

'And our Nursery?'

That was Mrs Sherry's cross voice, but Ted Edgeworth had two hours at Asda in front of him before he sat down, and he decided that he wasn't going to hear it. Irwell Valley Education Authority, Barton Wood Primary School and Headteacher Chris Sherry could wait until Monday morning.

He fiddled with the gate and waited. What was she doing now?

Chris Sherry finished copying the address from the sign and slammed the door of her car. She sped past the still-fiddling foreman and glanced down at her diary. *Glebe Lane*. Hadn't she been there this morning?

'Right, Mr Dunphy –' she said it out loud – 'you're the caretaker – take care!'

She almost smiled at that. Almost.

'Aaargh! Aaargh!' As Kenny screamed he felt a tickle all over his chest and stomach and found that it gave him the strength to pull himself up the cupboard shelves like a chimp at Chester Zoo. He banged wildly at the thick skylight and blazed his eyes into Miranda while he waited for the fire in his belly to burn itself out and leave him empty and exhausted. He knew all about that feeling – adrenalin – 'your emotionals', old Gran called it. And Kenny hated it – hated it. When you'd been through what he'd been through you knew your 'emotionals' all right.

He glared down again. Why wasn't *she* up here? Miranda? He banged again, and *'struth*! had to duck. The nut-hatch was throwing discs at him now. He banged the window fiercely to show her what to do.

'He's wasting all our breath,' she said to the doll.

Breath? Air? Oxygen? Miranda was right, he *was* wasting it. It was only a tiny cupboard, best to save it, save the oxygen. He took a huge breath and held it until he was purple. He tried one more bang on the window, turned round and exploded air as he caught a disc heading straight for his face: *'struth!* again. Any second these 'emotionals' were going to burst out of his chest.

★

Walk on, (clap, clap) *walk on,* (clap, clap)
With 'ope . . . in your heart
And you'll ne-ver walk . . . alone
You'll ne-ver walk . . . alone . . .

Patrick Dunphy added the sound effects of an Anfield full house and sent his sports bag skidding down the stairs – just as somebody rapped at the letter-box. He'd fix that bell when he got back from the match on Sunday.

'Door! Maureen – door!'

He banged his way into the bedroom and picked up his wallet, whistling as he checked the all important match tickets and the spending money he'd got out of the Building Society.

'Who is it, Maureen? . . . Maur?' Dunphy stopped whistling and listened. 'Maureen, who is it?'

Downstairs, Maureen Dunphy coughed before answering. 'It's, um, Mrs, er . . . Sherry.'

'Mrs Who?' Dunphy went to the top of the stairs. Mrs Sherry? *Sherry!* – with two hundred pounds of Barton Wood software lying on the telephone table?

'It's not a social call,' Chris Sherry announced.

You're telling me! Dunphy raced down the stairs, hoping he'd got his angles right and was blocking the view of the telephone table from the door.

CHAPTER FIVE

Kenny wedged his cheeks into the large gap under the steel door and, bog-eyed, signalled for Miranda to do the same. But she was still diving around, flinging discs, talking to that stupid doll. Funny, he thought, she didn't seem to be going purple, or anything. Anyhow, he was going to have to take charge.

'Got any money?' he asked.

'Course not.'

Kenny wriggled himself on to his back and fiddled in his pocket. 10p. That would do.

DING, DING, DING ... DONG, DONG, DONG ... DING, DING, DING. It didn't sound too good on the pipe, but SOS was SOS. Somebody might hear it. He banged again and felt his stomach rumble. 'We have our tea now,' he said, making his watch bleep. 'What time do you have yours?'

Miranda jumped from her shelf, looked down at him, and made no attempt to answer his question. 'Are you gonna ask to be bigger?'

Kenny looked up from his commando position and found himself face to face with the doll. Miranda was already climbing back up the shelf.

'You know,' she said, 'up in heaven.'

Kenny sat up and forgot about his breathing. Heaven? Did she think . . .? He stared at the girl, hard: who seemed calm enough, which in a way made it all the more scary.

'I'll be a nurse up there,' she said, 'if God wants.' And then suddenly she was shouting and Kenny couldn't stop himself from shrinking back. 'Better than living . . . stinkin' –' she hurled an empty disc box at the door – 'down –' she threw one at Kenny – 'here!'

Kenny scrambled for his coin and started hammering out his SOS on the pipe, but Miranda was already calm again.

'No one ain't coming. No one cares about me.'

Kenny thought of old Gran. She cared about *him*, and she'd be going spare. 'She'll have cooked it now – my tea.'

Miranda sniffed. 'Hate tea. Broke the leg off our chair 'smornin'.' At least she was answering. 'Mam's after me, don't want me home for no tea.'

'That why you wrecked that room, then?' Miranda only shrugged, and Kenny pushed his luck. 'So why d'you write "hat" on the wall?'

Miranda shrugged again – followed by another explosion, and Kenny made sure he was out of reach. '"Hat"? "Hate", you dilk! People don't write "hat" on walls,' she told him. 'Who's gonna write

47

"hat" on a wall?'

'You did. That was "hat" that you wrote; wasn't spelt right for "hate".'

'Hate spelling.'

'You need an "e" for "hate", "magic e",' he said, in between some breathing and more hammering. 'Didn't you have that programme at your other school – you know, Ozzie Owl?'

'Closed me eyes at programmes.'

Kenny broke into a half-remembered song.

> *'What makes a mat say "mate"? It's "E",*
> *What makes a bit say "bite"? It's "E",*
> *What makes a –'*

But he couldn't remember any more, so he spoke a finish. 'What makes "hat" say "hate"? It's –'

Miranda was suddenly on the floor and screaming. 'It's "EEEEEEEEEEEE!"' Then she spat, just missing Kenny, who wasn't too sure what she'd done.

'Erk! What's that, spit?'

'No!' she screeched. 'It's spite – with an "e"!'

Kenny stared at her, and then hammered on the door until his fists hurt.

With football songs still ringing round his head, Patrick Dunphy stomped down his front path and glared at his wife's pretty smile.

'Patrick's got his keys, he knows where his duty lies,' she'd said. Terrific! So he was on his way back into school when he should have been on his way

48

down the motorway. Liverpool–Tottenham in the fourth round of the Cup and a London night planned with the lads months ago. Terrific! *You'll never walk alone?* Old Sherry hadn't even offered him a lift round the corner.

He tapped his jeans pocket for the school keys and, more carefully, checked the package hidden inside his shirt. At least she hadn't spotted the discs – and now he'd have half a chance to get them back. Check all the locks, though! What a cheek on a Friday night: the place wasn't his responsibility till Monday. He tried to keep his anger going, but as he rounded the corner and came to the gleaming new door of the school, he had to fight to keep a proud smile off his lips. This was *his* school, and Maureen was right, he knew where his duty lay: and if that meant stopping another break-in, he'd stop it. London would wait for him: and the Reds wouldn't kick off without him there, would they? He gave his keys a jangle. Yes, he knew his duty, all right. People round here would soon see that he ran a tight ship. Oh yes, a very tight ship. And after a fumble and a drop he put the right key into the lock.

In the cupboard they'd heard the door. Immediately, Kenny had a shout in his throat and his fist drawn back for another door hammering: but Miranda was quicker even than that: she had his fist in her own and was squeezing like a python.

'Wanna get put away? We'll both get done for that mess in there!'

Kenny's eyes rolled, but a stinking hand over his mouth cut off his answer – and any chance of a yell.

'We ain't giving in till we have to! Hate giving in!' She hissed it into his ear. 'You keep your gob shut! And *you!*' she added, grabbing something from the shelf – and Kenny found himself staring into the wide blue eyes of the doll.

This was a nightmare! It had to be a nightmare! He'd wake up in a minute and there would be Gran with a cup of tea and a Bourbon biscuit. He closed his eyes and opened them again, hoping . . .

The light was fading fast by the time Lee saw the school door close behind the tall, red-haired woman. He came out of the bushes wearing the hard sneer he'd started using during the rows at home: before they'd moved to this new dump, just him and his mum. It was a useful sneer; it kept people out and his feelings in. Back then it had saved him having to let his mum and his dad know whose side he was on: now it would just make him look hard to that titch Kenny Bayfield. Hard, not worried: it wouldn't show that he was worried sick about losing that leather ball, the last thing his dad had given him before he left.

He knew he wasn't going to see Bayfield now, and as lights flickered on inside the school building he headed off towards home – only half a home these days – and slowly the sneer became worry, and then, as his house got nearer, the worry became real sadness.

★

'Half an hour won't make too much difference, will it? The motorways will be much clearer for one thing.'

Patrick Dunphy, walking a step behind the headteacher, rolled his eyes; and he'd only just got a normal look on to his face when she turned.

'What do you reckon?'

'Uhh?' Dunphy looked as blank as the brand new walls, while Mrs Sherry stared into him with a gaze so clear that he felt sure she knew what was inside his jacket and was only waiting for him to confess.

'What do you reckon, draw down there and bring them back to Anfield?'

'Oh! Er, yeah . . . I suppose . . .'

'Spurs' away form isn't up to much, is it?'

'No —' he said, his spirits suddenly on the up — she was talking football — 'but we'll thrash 'em down there!' She wasn't so bad, his new boss! And he felt really sorry for her when he saw the state of the Nursery.

'*Hat?*' he asked eventually.

'Hate.' The answer was routine for Mrs Sherry, and she was already checking how far the ooze of red paint had stretched across the floor. 'I'll see to this while you check the doors and windows.'

'Right.' Dunphy watched her move off — and as soon as she'd gone, ran on his toes in the opposite direction, the box of discs in one hand, keys in the other. He reckoned he'd got about a minute at the security cupboard before she got back. 'Come on!

Come on!' He couldn't find the key one-handed and he had to put the box down. Help, it seemed he'd used half his time just getting to here. 'Where are you, you little . . .?' And his fumbling fingers found it. 'There you are!'

The rattle in the lock seemed like the loudest noise Kenny had ever heard. He and Miranda and the doll were pressed against the wall, Miranda's hand hard over his mouth. Slowly, the door began to open: the banging inside Kenny's chest seemed to stop, and the grip on his mouth tightened. But there was no need for it now; forget the SOS tapping and the banging on the door – he wasn't after being found. Miranda was right, he didn't want the Juvenile Court.

There was light now, coming in, and Kenny closed his eyes as he waited for the angry, accusing face.

'I'll need some hot water, Mr Dunphy. Have you got a kettle?'

It was a woman's voice – the one who'd been here when he'd first hidden in the cupboard a thousand years ago. He jerked his head and caught Miranda's wild stare. Then there was a man's voice, centimetres away: loud – but sounding as panicky as Kenny felt.

'Er, in my room, yes.' A disc box or something skidded across the floor. 'On my way, Mrs Sherry . . .' And Kenny heard the rattle of keys going further away – with the shaft of light still there.

The door had been left open.

'"To boil a kettle and not have tea can only bring bad luck to thee . . ." One of me dear old mother's sayings.' Dunphy slurped his tea and, leaning against the wall, watched Mrs Sherry mop the paint which had run a lazy, destructive river out there into the corridor.

'As long as you're not in too much of a hurry to get on to the motorway!'

'Oh, no.' Dunphy pushed the door and kicked the bucket into the Nursery, her sarcasm wasted. 'I reckon you're right about the traffic, and . . . 'struth!' He stopped suddenly while the water slopped.

'What?' Mrs Sherry looked where he was looking.

Dripping down the wall, in gloriously fresh red paint, an 'e' had been added to the end of 'hat'.

'Oh, magic!' Dunphy said – and twisted at the sound of the school door slamming.

'Yes.' Mrs Sherry ignored the sound – whoever it was had gone. She looked at the wall and sighed. '"Magic e" – it looks like Barton Wood has taught its first lesson!'

CHAPTER SIX

Monday had come. The County Primary School was finally opening its doors to the children of Barton Wood. 'Welcome' said a sign in many languages. There was jostling in the doorway: bags were new and clothes were ironed. Faces still shone from rough flannels that morning and static hair still stood from hot baths the night before.

Just inside the entrance Mrs Swainsgate, the school secretary, was making a brave attempt at crowd control. 'No, no, there's no Nursery. Vandals, I'm afraid. Yes, tomorrow . . . Yes, yes . . . Year Five? Hall, dear . . . Yes, all Juniors, hall . . .' But there were just too many questions to answer; too many tense mothers, anxious fathers, crying toddlers. There were grid-locked push-chairs, and a dog; and, of course, there was Patrick Dunphy. Right in the middle of it all, Patrick Dunphy was up a ladder removing a section of the ceiling: and when he managed to pass it down to Mrs Swainsgate, the look on her Department Store Manager's face made all but the most foolhardy parent decide to try their luck in the hall, without the privilege of a personal word.

Inside the hall itself there was a church-like hush. The children, a new community, were less willing to speak once their parents had drifted away. Those who did know one another were happy to look around, seeing themselves on the new wallbars or out on the football pitch where there'd be 'real goals'. A few were looking at the smart hessian display-boards and remembering from their old schools the pride of a piece of work rewarded with a public showing.

Most of the older children – still sitting in their coats – were remembering instructions about making a good impression, and they eyed the adults in the hall with a careful attention. Who'd be teaching them? It didn't look as if they'd be having the smiling man who was getting the eight- and nine-year-olds together, and it couldn't be the young one with the smallest children. So would it be the tall woman in the suit – or that strict old-fashioned-looking one?

Lee Rayner wasn't bothered what sort of impression he made. His only concern was how to kick away the arm supporting Nicky Power and to see him collapse on the shiny floor. Esi Mensah wasn't concerned what impression she made, either. With eyes that had stolen the African sun of her ancestors, and a smile which reflected its warmth, Esi always made an impression, and she knew it. Standing by the wall and staring at some old-fashioned hunters in a painting by Brueghel, she was wondering why they were wearing motorbike helmets: everyone knew motorbikes and cars weren't invented in the old days. She looked round the hall for her mother – and saw her lecturing the man teacher, both of them looking cross.

'"See the head," the secretary said!'

'Yes,' Jack Higgins explained for the fifth time that morning, 'but I'm not the head. I'm the deputy. You need to see Mrs Sherry for enrolling.'

Mrs Mensah wasn't having it, but Mrs Sherry clapping her hands put an end to what little noise there was, and that went for her next bit of the argument. Everybody listened. Some, like Kenny Bayfield sitting next to Jordan Jenkins, trying so hard to look as if they were listening that they hardly heard what was being said. Lee and Nicky were the only people not watching the headteacher welcome everybody and give the usual stuff about a happy family and fresh starts: because Lee suddenly saw his chance to collapse Nicky just when Class One – that was them – were told that they would be taught by Mrs Clegg in the mornings and Mrs Sherry herself in the afternoons.

'Two teachers!' Jordan said. 'Meaning twice the trouble, Ken – or half!'

Five minutes later, and the same wide eyes that had taken in the hall were now devouring the new classrooms: six-sided tables, a carpet, work surfaces around the edges, and the sort of bare brick walls that looked good instead of run down. In Class One, even Nicky Power sounded impressed.

'Sorted, eh, Lee? Better than our other old dump!'

Lee was swinging back on his chair and fighting to get the sneer on to his face: Power should have known that you left all that 'positive' stuff for kids like this Jordan clown who went around with Bayfield.

There was a clap of hands from Mrs Clegg, barricaded behind her desk.

'Right, dear, sit down.' And Kompel, all smiles, got to her place. 'And you, dear, sit up!' Lee, in his own time, put his chair back on to four legs.

Class One's first day at Barton Wood School had begun.

'Right, Class One, I think we're nearly all . . .' But not quite. 'Anywhere, dear.'

David Kent had come in under the silent eyes of the class. He found the first empty seat and sat down, embarrassed, with Jordan and Kenny.

'And you are . . .?'

'David Kent, Miss.'

Mrs Clegg made a register note and looked over her glasses at the boy. 'And it's not "Miss", it's "Mrs Clegg".'

'Yes, Miss –'

'Pos-it-ive!' from Jordan, under his breath. She was a real old schoolmistress, this one: hair scragged back tight as if the twist at the back pulled her face into shape: and a look on it right now which said children tasted bad, real bad.

'– Mrs Clegg.'

'Now,' she was going on, 'is Miranda Pudsey here?'

Kenny knew the answer to that. His heart had started its thumping at just the thought of the girl, and he'd been keeping a weather eye out for her. 'Not here, Miss.'

'– es Clegg!' Lee Rayner had had to finish it, hadn't he? Kenny caught his smirking smile and saw him smash a fist into his palm. 'Where's my ball?' he was mouthing across the classroom. Kenny had wondered how long it would take. From the off that morning he'd kept well away from Rayner, gone to one side of the playground with his gran when the kid had gone to the other; sat at the front of the hall when Rayner had sat at the back; gone on this table in the classroom when Rayner had chosen his over there. But he knew he'd only ever been the bounce of a ball away from bother. He gripped the brand-new table and felt his fresh start drain its last away. There weren't new schools for kids like him. For kids like him any school was any school: and he hated them; he hated them all.

In her office, Mrs Sherry drew strength from a deep breath and looked up from her computer. It didn't take much to crowd her doorway, but right now you wouldn't get air through. It was filled with the departing Mrs Mensah and the incoming brooding menace of Mrs Pudsey, pulling a disinterested Miranda with her – and squeezing like a sparrow through them all came Gran Bayfield, holding an apple out in front of her like an egg through a rugby scrum.

'Sorry, sorry – it's my Kenny.' She mouthed the word *constipation*, but Kenny Bayfield's tummy problems were of no concern to Mrs Pudsey.

'We was next.'

'Sorry . . . of course. It's just his old tum. He needs his apple . . . you know.' She shielded this fact of life from Miranda. 'Helps him go . . .'

Mrs Sherry took the apple and Gran apologized again, edging out past the Pudseys. Miranda was shoved into the room, her piercing eyes taking it all in, the humming computer, the swivel chair . . . Mrs Pudsey followed her in, a hand still tight on the girl's collar.

'You want mischief?'

Mrs Sherry held out a welcoming hand.

'Sure? I'm Mrs Pudsey.'

'So –' Mrs Sherry smiled – 'you're Miranda.' Her face had the look of one who was remembering something important. 'You were having some extra help at your other school . . .?'

Mrs Pudsey broke in on the mental file-reading. 'Fat lot of help that was. She's still a little tyke!'

'Well,' Mrs Sherry said, her voice unchanged, 'we're getting some support for Miranda, someone to support her work in the classroom . . .'

'You'll need an armed guard for her, dear!'

'Oh, we want to be a lot more positive than that. Do you like computers, Miranda?'

'Hate 'em!' Miranda had sat on the swivel chair

at the headteacher's desk and, using a felt tip, was adding an 'e' to the end of every name on a class list.

Mrs Sherry left her to it; the list would have to be reprinted now, anyway. She squinted at the computer screen in front of her. 'No, I'm not too keen, but everything has to go into them these days. Now –' she tapped a key and turned to Miranda – 'could I just check your address, love?'

Miranda spun herself round in the leather chair. 'Twenty-three Glebe Lane,' she said, pointing to the words on the screen, 'with two of them "magic e's".'

Mrs Sherry stared hard at Miranda, at her face, and at the splashes of red paint on her dirty shell suit: she looked at the faint traces of red paint still on her own scrubbed skin from Friday night.

'Right, where d'you want her, then?' Mrs Pudsey was moving to be off; but, again, the doorway was blocked. In it was a large smiling man in a smart blazer, and trousers with razor-blade creases. Mrs Swainsgate was behind him mouthing apologies as he lifted an imaginary hat.

'Morning all. Thought I'd pop in.'

Mrs Sherry looked as if she were about to say something, or stop herself saying something: she knocked a felt tip on the floor and came up smiling. It was Len Bamber, local councillor, ex England footballer, and not only the Chair of Governors but the person whose pet scheme this school had been.

'Couldn't let things start wi'out wishing my school a good kick off.'

Mrs Sherry got up and shook his hand, busily. 'Well, I haven't got much time, but –' She said a brisk goodbye to Mrs Pudsey and gave Miranda's enrolment form to the secretary. 'Miranda's for Class One, then please continue with admissions.' She smiled like a polite and unruffled headteacher who had not been taken by surprise. 'I'm just going to show Councillor Bamber around *our* school.'

Lee was measuring rulers, and once he had checked that no one had a bigger one than his own, he was giving them out. Kompel was vigorously tapping the seat next to hers and signalling for Esi to come and sit there.

'Oooh, hold me hand at playtime!' Nicky said, but Kompel didn't care; a nice school, new work, someone friendly to sit with, and only one table away, David Kent! This was what 'happy' meant.

'Esi Mensah?' Mrs Clegg tried a smile.

'Yes, Miss?'

'*Missus Clegg!*' crowed the class.

The teacher coughed and nodded her approval like a pantomime Dame at a quick-learning audience. She shuffled some papers in front of her. 'OK, children, your first piece of work for me is this – um – sheet.' She held one out at arm's length, gave the quickest of looks over her shoulder at the blackboard of Maths she'd put up. 'It's a data – um – base. Mr Higgins's idea. Apparently, you put information about yourself on the sheet, add to it a picture of your beautiful faces, and then we bury all the information in a chest on Thursday or Friday. Some sort of time capsule thing . . .'

Lee Rayner didn't sound any more enthusiastic than she did. 'What's the point of doing work to bury it, Miss?'

She didn't have an answer. 'It's Mr Higgins's bright idea, so let's get on with it. Then you can do some real work.' She gave the papers to Sandra who, living up to her goalkeeping image, dropped them before giving them out.

As ever, the spirit-duplicated sheets were smelt by each child before carefully written names were added. Mrs Clegg sniffed at them, too, but at the questions, not the paper.

The sheets required details about each child from age, weight and height to favourite football teams and pop groups: altogether, not as rigorous as her board of sums: but at least the class was busy, and quiet. She walked around, admired Kenny's self-portrait, saw some children co-operating nicely in finding their heights and weights, began to look a little more relaxed. Until the door banged open and a girl stood there, staring in; someone in a shell suit. Mrs Clegg reached for the register.

'Miranda? Miranda Pudsey?'

'Yeah?'

The girl came in and went straight to the crate of milks. She took a bottle and stuffed in six straws before sitting on an empty desk to drink it.

'Yeah – *what*?' was all the teacher could say at first. But although the woman had her little ways, she was a skilled handler of children, and she quickly explained that, of course, all of them could choose when to have their milk.

Most had it then, and from there it was a step to seat Miranda and get her looking at a worksheet. Which was as well, because almost directly a visitor came in through the door as if he owned the place. The Chair of Governors, with Mrs Sherry.

'What a lovely quiet classroom, Mrs Clegg. This is the top class,' the headteacher told the councillor. 'Years Five and Six – low numbers, yet, but –'

'Oh, we'll grow. New folks moving in all't time: we shall be bustin' our zips 'fore we know it!' He laughed, waved his hand at the children, interrupted work.

Mrs Sherry waved a hand, too, at the modern tables, the lockers, the well-stocked library corner. 'Well, you certainly pulled the right strings to set us up, Mr Bamber. Classrooms very well designed – and cleverly connected to each other through these screens.' She pulled open a plastic curtain to reveal the younger Junior class of children on the other side: hard at work with John 'Jack' Higgins the deputy head crouching at a table and laughing at the 'Favourite Joke' section of someone's data sheet. He got up and walked through to shake hands with Len Bamber.

'Good morning, Mr Bamber.'

'Morning, lad.'

Mrs Clegg, arms folded, said it all with her face: what she reckoned to a classroom separated from

the next by no more than a sheet of plastic curtain.
She turned away from the strong handshake going
on and knelt herself down by Miranda. The girl
had done no writing on her data sheet but had
filled the 'Self-portrait' section with a picture of a
house.

'That's lovely, dear, but I think what we need
here is a picture of you – so we can bury it.'

'Bury it?' Len Bamber stopped his gazing round
and nodding, and was back to see what that was all
about.

Mrs Sherry explained. 'This is Jack's idea. The
children are filling in data sheets, lots of information
about themselves. The sheets are going to get
printed on our computers and then buried in a
treasure chest with bits and bobs from the 1990s.
Then, in a hundred years, Barton Wood pupils can
dig up the chest and remember the very first children who attended the school.'

'Oh, that's grand! School weren't like this in my
day.' Councillor Bamber gave Jack Higgins a huge
slap on the back. 'Splendid, Jack!'

'I only draw 'ouses!' Miranda was telling Mrs
Clegg.

Mrs Sherry knelt to her. 'Well, that's OK, Miranda, but what about *you*? The children in a hundred years' time won't know what you looked like,
will they?' She picked up David Kent's carefully
drawn portrait. 'See, they'll know all about
David . . .'

'I only draw 'ouses!' Miranda said again, and

grabbing a black crayon she hammered it down on to her picture. The crayon disintegrated. 'Hate colouring!'

Mrs Sherry put a hand on her shoulder. 'Well, what about a photo, then? Bring in a snapshot of yourself.'

'Ain't got none.'

But Sandra had. 'Oh, wicked! Photos! Can we all bring 'em, Miss? This drawing don't look like me.'

'No, looks like our dog!' From Lee.

'Woof-woof!'

Mrs Sherry put up quick hands in surrender. 'Well, I suppose so; but we'll have to do copies of them – we can't bury the real ones, your parents would be furious.'

Esi Mensah was sitting back on her chair, smiling. She had just looked across to the table by the wall where Jordan was drawing a moustache on Kenny Bayfield's self-portrait. She liked the look of old Jordan; he was a bit of fun, all his *pos-it-ive* stuff – and she reckoned she had just the photo at home to bring in and let him and the others see. It had been taken in Ghana, the last time the family had gone out; and it had her in traditional clothes for a little cousin's christening: a beautiful long dress and matching headscarf: and if she said it herself, she looked very tasty in that . . .

Playtime suddenly interrupted work, and private thoughts. Councillor Bamber and Mrs Sherry watched as the classes rushed out to test the new playground and run round those new markings sprayed on to the asphalt. Except Kenny. Kenny wasn't rushing for the playground where Lee and Nicky didn't have a ball to kick. He saw Miranda still sitting and hammer-crayoning her picture, and no one was sending her out: so he quietly carried on with his own, starting by rubbing out Jordan's moustache. He hated himself for it: but he also hated playgrounds: they could be very dangerous places . . .

'Why don't you fill in one of our sheets, Mr Bamber?' Mr Higgins was offering the man one. 'Go down in history with the rest of us?'

'Aye, I'll do that.' Councillor Bamber pulled out a gold fountain-pen and laid it on the desk while he looked over the data sheet. 'This is good, eh, lass? Though I don't think your computer would print my Favourite Joke!'

He laughed at his own humour as Miranda saw the pen on the desk in front of her.

'That's our only problem,' Mr Higgins was saying. 'Our printers haven't arrived yet . . .' His voice tailed as Miranda lifted the gold fountain-pen ready to hammer it down on her already obliterated house. He grabbed it from her in mid-air, handed it with a smile to Len Bamber.

'Oi!' she said.

'So –' the Chair of Governors autographed the top of his sheet with a flourish from years of practice – 'our kiddies won't see their work printed; that's a shame, lad.'

Mrs Sherry shot her deputy a glare that would have frozen molten lava.

'I've got an idea!' Jack Higgins coughed. 'Old Bob Guest over the canal – head of St Paul's – he'll likely lend us a printer.'

With hardened eyes, Mrs Sherry watched her deputy get another clap on the back.

'Excellent, lad! I know Bob Guest – runs the best football team around. He'll help out if you've not got yourselves organized yet.'

Mrs Sherry was white now, Higgins red.

'Great, this, Jack!' Len Bamber put an arm on each of their shoulders. 'Tell you what – let's make an occasion of burying this chest thingummy. I'll come along with my official silver spade an' we'll make it a big do, eh? Smashing!' He rubbed his hands.

'Yes, smashing, Jack!' said Mrs Sherry from the side of her mouth, staring at Kenny sitting there but not seeing him.

'I'll go and watch the children lining up.' Jack Higgins manoeuvred round a couple of chairs and got out of the room, fast: and just for a moment Kenny thought he recognized a certain look on the teacher's face, a look Kenny always seemed to have on his own.

But, no, he thought, he's a man – he's not got nothing to worry about.

CHAPTER SEVEN

Kenny had survived the morning. He'd finished his data sheet and in a new yellow Maths book he'd carefully worked his way through Mrs Clegg's board of sums. He'd done all right there – only the table with Kompel and that girl who kept looking over here at Jordan had got further. And David Kent. But things were never as sweet as just getting your work done. At twelve o'clock it was dinnertime – and there was no escape like he'd managed at playtime.

Sitting in the school hall, he left most of his lukewarm Sausage Surprise and French Fries and tried telling the dinner-lady that he'd got work to finish in class: but Mrs Smart was having none of that.

'Oh no – no children on their own in the building: Mrs Sherry's rules, love.'

So he had to face the outside. And it was only two steps into the playground before there was a weight on his shoulder and a hand round his neck. Kenny swore at himself: he'd got rusty. When the normal teachers weren't there the playground was a jungle – and he'd forgotten his survival skills. You stuck within view of a dinner-lady at all times. If he'd been thinking straight he'd have taken more time over his afters and offered to help Mrs Smart with wiping the tables – until she got out here. But now he couldn't think straight – and the squeezing round his neck was making blue and gold dots flash behind his eyelids.

'My ball, Scum – now!'

There was a bad pain in his arm as Lee Rayner forced it right up his back. Kenny could kick – but was it best to wait a bit before he jacked this up into a real fight? He sucked in breath, somehow, felt the bony forearm pressing in hard on his throat. He'd have to make some move . . .

'Ey! Let go of his neck!' Jordan had come stepping over. 'You heard – let go!'

Lee let go. He didn't fancy the off with Jordan, then. But he wasn't running out of threats. 'That ball, Midget!'

Jordan replaced Lee's arm with his own, round Kenny's shoulder: no pressure. 'Come on, Kenny boy, let's ask that caretaker bloke.'

'You better pray you get it, Scud!'

Inside the building they found the caretaker's office, not far from the front entrance to the school. *Mr P. Dunphy – Premises Management* it said on a notice – in Gothic script from one of the computer programs. They guessed it meant 'caretaker' and knocked on the door.

'Come!'

Kenny was in just before Mr Dunphy could switch his miniature television from *Sesame Street* to the lunch-time news: he was eating from a packet of sandwiches, sitting up at a work-bench. Kenny told him about wanting Lee's ball back, please.

'You wait outside and I'll see what I can do.'

'But –' Kenny couldn't go out there again without the ball. Lee might have got organized to sort out him and Jordan.

'Don't give me any buts. I stand no nonsense with balls, you'd better all learn that.' He waved a ham and pickle at Kenny. 'Right outside, in the playground, I'll be out.'

The wait in the playground had them all there together – most of Class One who wanted football: with a tight grip on Kenny's anorak hood by Lee Rayner. They stood outside the school door like a crowd waiting for a star: and at last a silhouette on the glass turned into Patrick Dunphy. Out he came holding Lee's casey high above his head. There were shouts and cheers, but he stood, like the Statue of Liberty, awaiting silence.

'Now, boys and girls,' he said solemnly, 'I'm not going to give you back this fine leather football . . .'

More shouts, less excited, a load of *Not fairs*. Kenny's hood was twisted hard, lifting him up on to his toes with the top of his zip pressed into his Adam's apple.

'You're not getting this ball back . . . unless you

can get it off me!' And Dunphy dropped the ball at his feet and dribbled fast across the playground. Lee let go and joined the screaming crowd who followed the swerving figure as he went towards the boundary, doing his own television commentary. 'And it's Barnes, Barnes . . . He finds Rush . . . back to Barnes and –' Dunphy skied it: right over the fence.

Kenny, high on fear, relief, excitement, wanted to laugh. They couldn't blame him for that.

'And it's gone into the Kop. Barnes goes to retrieve it . . .' Dunphy, as red as a Liverpool scarf, ran round to the gate, leaving the runners who'd kept up with him in something of a frustrated huddle. 'Won't be a minute – read your match programmes!'

'He'll get it,' said Lee: and in case anyone spotted his real relief at seeing his ball again, he put on his sneer for those near him. 'Anyhow, got something for a bit of fun 'safternoon . . .' He reached into a pocket and pulled out a big plastic spider – a good one, realistic: Nicky, Kenny, Jordan, they all backed off it at first.

'Gonna put it in the register. Give Old Mother Clegg something more to worry about than getting called "Miss" all the time.'

'Pure!' said Nicky.

'But we haven't –' said Kenny.

'Shuddup, chicken! Look to my casey,' he told Nicky – and running round a dinner-lady chasing Miranda Pudsey, Lee went off at a crouch into the school.

Dunphy came back with the ball and Nicky went to get it; while Kenny looked at Jordan, and Jordan looked at Kenny and did a quick high five. They nodded at one another. This afternoon was going to be a bit of fun, which Kenny reckoned he could enjoy . . .

The bundle outside Class One was a noisy one, and Mrs Sherry's attention was taken by the posse of dinner-ladies who had brought Miranda to her to face justice.

'Thank you, I'll deal with her now. And football has finished, so quietly, you people, in you go.'

'Got it!' Jack Higgins called over the heads, coming in through the hall and lifting a St Paul's printer for Mrs Sherry to see.

'Good. That'll please Councillor Bamber. I've chased them up about ours – they should be here to-morrow!'

'Ah.' Jack Higgins joined the end of the line of children going in, and stopped at Mrs Sherry. 'Er – there is one thing . . . Well, you know what Bob Guest is like . . .'

'No.' It was a snap.

'He wants St Paul's to play us.' Higgins coughed, waited, weighed the printer.

'Play us at what, for goodness' sake? This is our first day.'

Sandra was in between them. 'Miss, tell Nicky, Miss . . .'

'Well, at, um, football.'

Sandra forgot her injury. 'Football! Football! We've got a football match!' she shouted into the room.

'Not so fast! We'll see.'

But the class was celebrating, and Sandra was tugging at the sleeve of Mrs Sherry's blouse. 'Miss, Miss . . . Can girls play, Miss?'

'Of course!' Which was what Mrs Sherry thought about the only-boys-for-football nonsense: but the class took it to mean the OK for the match. The cheers were loud, and Mrs Sherry knew when to give in. 'Well, it looks like I'm outvoted.' Another cheer – and a quick bid to be captain from Lee. 'But one more word about football and it's off. Off ! Do you understand?'

The class did understand, and folded arms and straightened backs said so. Jack Higgins was dismissed with a very straight 'thank you', and Mrs Sherry headed for the register. Now the football hush was deepened by anticipation. Everyone knew what was inside the register.

'Right, register, then we'll do some English, and to finish off your first day we'll have some drama.'

'We'll have some drama all right,' a low voice predicted.

Lee had already realized the mistake he'd made. Not listening that morning, he hadn't got it into his head that Mrs Clegg wouldn't be here. There was a deathly silence led by him as Mrs Sherry perched herself on the desk, opened the heavy green register, and let the daylight on to his large, realistic spider.

Gasps, shudders, some well-prepared screams – and some real ones from those who hadn't seen the thing at dinner-time.

'A spider!'

'Help!'

'Does it bite?'

'Mum!'

Chairs scuttled, people moved back: but Mrs Sherry didn't even blink.

'Ah,' she said, '*Araneus diadematus*. Not a bad model.' She looked up to where the other half of the stares were going. 'Thank you, Lee. My husband works with creatures like these.'

Lee looked for words, and found them. 'He can have it, Miss.'

'How very kind. Now, where shall I keep it?'

'Bury it in the treasure chest, Miss. Pos-it-ive!'

'Keep it away from my photo!' Esi hunched her shoulders for Jordan.

'Oh, we'll do that. But not a bad idea.' Mrs Sherry brought the incident to a close, no blood on the floor. 'Although I can't bury it with the treasure chest because Councillor Bamber would run a mile if it jumped out on him!' After the laugh she took the talk back to their work, and the historic day they'd have on Friday when their data went under the ground. And Kenny sat there not sure whether he was pleased or sorry that Lee Rayner hadn't caught it in the neck for the stunt he'd pulled.

Esi was a girl with only happiness in her heart on

that first Friday morning. Held hard in her hand, not even trusted inside her EuroDisney rucksack, was the family photo-album. She'd brought the whole thing, jammed full of photographs of herself and the family from their Ghana trip for the christening: precious, but she'd sworn she'd get it back home safe and sound, she'd sworn her life on that. What she reckoned was, having the whole album would give Jordan Jenkins the chance to pick out her best photo for the copying and the burial. She'd like him to do that.

But things didn't work out as planned. They were all admiring the album at first, her sitting up in her place, straight-backed and proud as those aunties and cousins she'd met out in Africa.

'Oh, they're lovely, Es,' from Kompel.

'Wow! Where was this took?' from Sandra.

'Oh, how beautiful, Esi, what a lovely costume,' from Mrs Clegg.

Then Kenny and Jordan came over and she took a deep breath. Jordan was about to speak. He looked her in the eyes, reached into his bag and pulled out an album of his own. 'Pos-it-ive!' he said. 'Got a swap for Gazza?' And he threw a football sticker on top of her photos.

In the end Mrs Swainsgate helped her choose: a pretty picture where the headscarf showed itself off and made her eyes big and sparkly. The secretary took the album and went to make a photocopy.

There was a short assembly in which Mrs Sherry showed everyone the magnificent treasure chest which Mr Higgins's class had designed and Mr Fielding, one of the parents, had made. She explained why they had to have a plastic picnic box inside– *non biodegradable* – and she warned them to have their data sheets and any artefacts ready for burial by five minutes to ten. Esi would have to be quick getting that photocopy stuck to her paper. Back in the classroom Mrs Clegg was short-tempered in all the hectic waving of data sheets and the scramble to fill in last minute details: Esi had an eye to the door all the while, but Mrs Swainsgate brought back the album and the photocopy with the dinner-money change.

'Can I borrow this outfit for my next Ladies' Night?' she asked. Esi hoped she wasn't serious. 'Now, I'm putting this album on your teacher's desk for safe keeping. I doubt you can just pop over to Africa to get these pictures taken again!'

Esi shook her head and got to work with her glue stick. She had the picture stuck on just as Mrs Clegg clapped her hands.

'Has anybody not yet handed in their sheet?'

Esi smoothed her picture down and took it out to the desk. She saw her album safely there and put her data sheet on the pile next to it. She looked at her chosen picture, smiled, and wondered if anyone would think she was pretty in a hundred years' time.

'Come on, final chance!' And it would be, with Mrs Clegg! There was a scraping of chairs and Lee and Nicky, coming away from some murky business of their own, went last minute to their trays and pulled out their sheets, threw them on to the desk. But it was Sandra, last of all with everything as usual, who put her sheet on the very top of the untidy, spreading pile. She smiled at Mrs Clegg, who nodded her approval at her as she put everything into some sort of order.

'OK, everybody!' Mrs Sherry was in the doorway with the plastic picnic hamper. 'Five minutes until the chest is buried for a hundred years! Artefacts, data sheets, please . . .'

Kompel collected up the ballpoint pens, the newspapers, the plastic football and the cheap digital watch that the class had decided to bury in the box. Sandra carried the pile of data sheets over to Mrs Sherry, and she put them on top.

'Mr Bamber's all ready now, Mrs Clegg.'

Mrs Clegg gave instructions for the class to line up at the door.

'She'd get you in that box, Titch!' Lee was right behind Kenny.

Kenny turned to his tormentor, wasn't sure what he'd do, but it could have been something he'd regret – except David Kent held him back. 'Easy, Ken!'

'Don't fret, Kenny boy. It's what's in here what counts!' Jordan thumped his own chest. 'I tell you: be pos–it–ive!'

Quickly, the line sorted itself out while Kenny's lump in the throat went down. There were times when he wouldn't mind going under with that box, and he wasn't joking . . .

'Come on at the back there, we shall miss it! And don't leave any valuables, the door's not locked . . .'

The line went out – while Esi fought the flow to get back into the room. She'd got valuables in there. Mother, did she have valuables in there . . .!

In the room Miranda was still sitting at her place. 'Like it here when it's quiet.'

'Yeah.' Esi hurried to the desk. Good job she'd come back in, then. She didn't trust Miranda, not with her valuable album still here. She got to the front and took a look, and then she closed her eyes. She breathed in deeply and she looked again, checked calmly what she had not seen.

The album was not on the desk. It wasn't on the desk, and it wasn't in the drawer. She scrabbled round further. It wasn't on the seat, and it wasn't on the floor. It wasn't in the bin. And it was nowhere near Miranda. It wasn't in the room.

Esi rushed to the window and she banged and banged. The field was right outside – and there was that big man who'd come round the school on Monday. He was hitting the ground with a silver spade, and there was Mr Dunphy taking a video of it and there was Mrs Sherry and everybody, all out there clapping.

The hole had been dug ready, and now the chest was buried.

Esi banged again, and shouted. 'The box! It's in the box! No! Oh no!'

But they were all so busy with their clapping and being sure they were on the video that no one heard her and no one saw her. It was like being in a big wave and everyone on the beach was just carrying on.

'No!' she screamed.

Miranda wandered over to the window. 'What's up with you?'

'My album! My family album! It's in the treasure chest!'

Miranda shrugged, and went back to the house she was drawing. 'No sweat – get it back in 'undred years!'

Esi stared out, and everything out there seemed to freeze as great silver tears slid down her face; while the sound of her sobbing seemed to drown completely the sounds of cheering that were ringing round the school.

CHAPTER EIGHT

Jordan Jenkins came back into school and stood making up his mind on the front mat. Schools had that dead feel once the kids had gone, spooky; it had him all two-minded about whether to look for Mr Dunphy or just go for what he wanted: which left his feet staying where they were while his head cocked round a corner, listening for a vacuum on a classroom carpet, some sound of normal life. But what suddenly caught him was a laugh coming from the staffroom, a party sort of laugh. He stood very still and waited for it to come again – but all he got was silence, like they were telling secrets, or watching something. So he stayed where he was while he plucked up the guts to go knocking on their door; or to run on into the empty school.

Behind the closed door Mrs Sherry's eyes were like a doll's, staring at nothing, as if she were thinking there could only be one thing worse than watching someone's home video and that was watching someone's *bad* home video. And the rest of the staff were propped around like soft toys in a cot while Patrick Dunphy's recording of the burial zoomed in and zoomed out and raked from side to side. He held no one in the picture for the time it took the eye to focus before the camera was swung round in some other direction, so they all stared vacantly at the screen with their heads held back, only sharpening up when the Infants' teacher held the wine box over their glasses. All the same, it was good to relax after Councillor Bamber's storming performance, good to be a school staff laughing together after their first public event.

'Brought his own silver spade!'

'He's used to these ceremonies.'

'I bet he declares his front door open every time he goes inside!'

'Anyhow, it was a good project, Jack, really good for the kids.' Mrs Sherry leaned over and patted Mr Higgins on the back, public thanks.

'Not original,' Jack said, 'burying something.'

'They do it over the cemetery every day!' Patrick Dunphy boom-boomed at his own joke and rested his leg over the arm of the chair like a man who felt at home: and he took it off double quick at a sudden loud knock on the staffroom door. The sound of it, it had to be either Councillor Bamber returned, or Black Rod from Parliament.

Mrs Sherry opened the door, eyes ready for either – to Jordan.

'I forgot my picture.'

Mrs Sherry could sometimes give people a sharp poke just by looking at them.

'Sorry, Miss.'

'Where is it?'

'In my tray.'

She jerked her head in the direction of Jordan's classroom, and Jordan went. But halfway across the empty hall he slowed down. Kids always said there was a ghost in every school, except he didn't believe in ghosts: except you never knew . . . It was a fair old way from the others, over here, and he didn't know whether to tiptoe all quiet into the classroom or do a quick run and snatch. He went for the snatch. Shouting 'Pos-it-ive! Pos-it-ive! Pos-it-ive!' to scare off any spooks, he ran into the classroom, grabbed his picture from his tray, grabbed again because he hadn't got hold of it at all, and was turning to get off out when he suddenly heard this ghostly moan. An electric shock crackled up his spine and tried to uncurl his hair.

It had come from over in the corner – he wanted away from there like a Mustang from the lights, except there was no way he could spark a nerve to get anything moving, not an arm, not a leg, not a foot. He stared into the gloomy space not even trying a shout.

And the noise came again; but this time not so much a moan as a cry; and when he listened not a ghostly cry, but a hurt kid cry. Which gave him the courage to look to see who it was over there, huddled on the carpet.

It was Esi: and as he looked she cried some more and she started rocking herself like someone with a really bad pain.

'Esi! What's up?'

'They're gonna kill me!'

A flash of that old ghost came back. 'Who are? Where?' Jordan's eyes were all round the room at once.

'My mum and dad.'

'Oh.' Being killed by her mum and dad – that was all. 'Kill you for what?'

Esi looked up at him like some pathetic victim. She pointed to the photograph Jordan had come to get. 'Our album, our ... family album. It got buried, in the chest.'

'No it never.' He turned away from her. She was daft. 'They took photocopies for burying, stupid!'

But she was back to having her face pressed against the carpet, and it was hard to hear what she was mumbling. 'Mine ... got ... buried ... in with the books and papers. Got put in a pile that got buried, I know it did. It was on there, wasn't it?' She pointed behind her, anywhere, but she meant the teachers' desk where all the bits and pieces had been. 'I can't go home without it. They only lent it for the day – pain of death.'

Life had come back to Jordan's limbs; and he crouched to put his arms round the girl: what he would have done for an Infant, or a cat – being kind, stopping the crying. But as he was bent there he smelt the sweet perfume of her hair; and he gave her a little hug. 'I'll take you home.' He turned the hug into a shake, in case she got the wrong idea. 'Listen – they're all still there, getting drunk. You gotta tell 'em – an' we'll make 'em dig it up. Stupid! Got no option, have they?' He shook her again, but more gently – and he didn't mean 'stupid'. He pulled her up, and she came with him.

'I had to . . . guard . . . that album . . . with my life.' She was still having to speak between deep breaths, like a baby with hiccups.

'An' you looked great in that African head-thing. We'll get it back. Trust old Jordan. Be pos-it-ive!' And he led her by the hand, out of the classroom and across the hall.

When he made the announcement in the staff-room doorway it was as if the wine they'd been drinking had suddenly turned to water. Ice cold water.

'What?'

'It's not true!'

'Ye gods and little fishes!'

Mrs Sherry took a look at her wrist in case it was the first of April before she started checking Esi's story – where the album had been, how it could have got put in the pile that had to be buried, why it was so valuable. But when the classroom had also been checked there was no way round it, it had to be believed – the album was buried in the chest and would have to be dug up before Esi could go home that afternoon.

Patrick Dunphy and Jack Higgins did the digging while the staffroom was put back to rights and the door shut quietly on the day. And the album was found, handed up to Esi without a word by the care-taker.

'Thank you.' And a huge swallow. Esi clutched the album to her; cold, but not damp and no harm done. A last big sob. 'Thank you.'

The chest was not reburied: Mrs Sherry was very straight on the fact that the children would have to know what had happened – without mentioning any names, of course.

Jordan kept his word and walked Esi home, Esi gripping her album tight. She stopped at her gate.

'Ta, Jordan, thanks a mill!'

''S all right.' Jordan was going on, wasn't one to hang about: when out of nowhere he was being kissed on the cheek, and more than an auntie's peck. 'Ey!' He wiped it off – and was somehow sorry she saw him do that: went on just a couple of steps while he thought of something special to say. 'You wanna wear that head-thing to school,' he told her. 'You look wicked in that.'

Esi watched him till he'd turned the corner.

'You been kept back for something? I've got two new babies over Pennington. I'm off out soon as your daddy comes in.' Mrs Mensah had the door open, a district nurse with calls to make. Seth, who was four, was in and out between her legs and bashing at Esi with a rattly balloon. None of which stopped Esi from putting the album on the hall table like a crown on to a cushion, really slow. Her mother would never know, but that album had taken some bringing home.

'They was pleased with the pictures, picked that one at the christening, all in my long dress and head-scarf . . .'

'That was my pick, an' all.' Mrs Mensah watched the girl go floating up to her bedroom.

It was a new bedroom, where Esi was still enjoying the treat of not having Seth the other side of a small rug, bossing it. She could read in here without putting up all sorts of barricades round the light, she could put her foot on the floor without going for a ride on a truck, and she had all the new wardrobe to herself. The soft toys round her pillow were all hers, and they were lying there in the order she wanted, with favourites either side of her head, and they wouldn't be hijacked by Seth for dropping down the stairs or throwing at the cat. It was her room, but it wasn't until she opened the wardrobe door that who she was started to show. Up to now the things on her walls were framed prints of butterflies and flowers, none of them hers, and the walls were too new for poster-sticking yet. But inside the wardrobe hung the long and beautiful Ghanaian christening dress they'd all admired, and round the top of the hanger was the headscarf which made her look so special – the headscarf Jordan had told her she'd look wicked in, wearing to school.

Esi took the dress from the wardrobe, held it up against her for quick acclaim from the mirror, and laid it down the length of her bed, like a princess reclining. The headscarf she put slowly on her head, used the mirror to get it just the same as Jordan had liked, and then stood there in front of the glass, close to.

'Pos-it-ive!' she said quietly.

'Very nice, an' all.'

She turned as quick as the click of a camera. Her mother was in the doorway, with Seth fighting to get through her legs.

'You mind what you're doing, missus. We'll be needing that when brother George comes over. Don't grow on trees, them dresses.'

Which Esi knew. This dress and the matching headscarf had been specially made in Ghana, and there was no repeating it here in Lancashire. And just as Seth made it into the room, she had the headscarf off and the dress back into the wardrobe.

'An' what's this "pos-it-ive"? Some other thing new off the telly?'

Esi shook her head. 'Course not.' She muffled her head in starting a romp with Seth: no way was she trusting her eyes looking up, not till her mother had gone out of the room.

On the new Barton Wood estate as well as over the canal in the older streets, parents were split between wanting the historic church school for their kids or the up-to-the-minute modern place. Two rival schools in the area, and now they were about to play one another in the football match Mr Higgins had got himself trapped into. So it was only natural that the Barton Wood players were getting to school early and staying late at the end of the afternoon – practising. They wanted to do themselves more than proud: it was a matter of making their parents right.

Before school on the Monday morning after the burial (and the digging up) of the treasure chest, the squad was working in pairs and groups on the playground. Mr Higgins was there with notebook in hand, running along the asphalt in a passing movement with David Kent: while Lee and Nicky, Billy Smith, Kompel and Sandra were practising passes and throw-ins. The shouts and the jargon all had that professional edge – which soon frightened off any early Infants – and it could have been some big club's training ground running up to a major cup-tie. Jack Higgins kept emphasizing it was only a friendly, nothing like the league stuff St Paul's played in – but among the squad there was no time for smiles, it was all in earnest. As the sun shone down white like an early floodlight, Jack Higgins stretched his legs to take a return ball placed just a metre in front of him. 'Good ball!' he shouted, but stretched a sinew too far in running on to it. 'Ooooee!' Over he went on the grass verge, in that way the slightly too old always go: careful and slow as they fall.

'Ups-a-daisy!' Lee Rayner was to him first, trying to pull him up.

'Sorry, Sir. You all right?' David Kent gave a hand.

'I'm too old for this.'

'No, you ain't, not really. It was a duff ball from Kent.'

'It was a good ball, should've got to it.' With their help Mr Higgins got up to hobble back on to the tarmac.

'Hospital ball!'

'Leave it, Lee. You get on while I put a wet paper-towel on this.' Mr Higgins limped off to applause, leaving the practising footballers to do their own thing: which, in Lee Rayner's case, was to start picking the offical team, pushing people about and lining them up like the Red Arrows.

'He won't want you to pick it.' Kompel bounced a ball the other way. 'Waste of time, we could be practising.'

'He don't know us, does he? He'll be chuffed I've done the business for him.' He pulled Sandra Smith into the rear position, in goal. 'You're here.' He put Kompel in front of her. 'You're here, back four.'

'You can't have one as the back four!' David Kent had folded his arms.

'I'll be back one, I don't mind. Long as we get playing. I'm cold. Anyway,' Kompel jogged out of position, and back, 'it's stupid this early, there's still people not here.'

'Who's not here?' Lee's counts always started and ended with Lee Rayner: all this was really about was setting up who was going to be captain.

'Kenny's not here,' David said. 'And Jordan.' He gave an eyes-to-heaven for Kompel; it was rotten when the teachers weren't about to stop this sort of thing.

'Midfield, them,' said Lee. 'They'll go in there.'

'And Esi, she's not here.' Kompel jogged out of place again.

'Oh, Esi! Large helpings!' Nicky turned on her

from where he'd put himself in the line-up, up front, twin striker. 'She'll make a difference, won't she? We ain't playing Barton Wood Girl Guides!'

'It's only a friendly . . .'

'No such thing!'

And for a moment they stood like an official silence while they all thought about that.

And there was a moment's silence going on in Esi's house: Seth looking for the toy in his cereal and their mother – getting over a bad night with one of the new babies in Pennington – wrapped in a thick dressing-gown and her own thoughts. Upstairs in her room, Esi was ready for school, and open on the bed was the EuroDisney bag she'd be taking. She said something she wouldn't want her mother to hear softly under her breath, because whenever she wanted quiet she never got it: and when she wanted a bit of noise, like right now, the whole house went silent prayer time. As carefully as she could – already she knew which one was the give-away floorboard – she crossed to her bedroom door and slowly, very slowly, she closed it. What she didn't want was any walking in on her, like her pos-it-ive moment the other night: and big woman nothing, her mother was wicked at silent walking. Esi was about to do something to please old Jordan, and that was private. She took the slow, safe route back to her bed – and with a last look round at the door she took a reach at her pillow and pulled something out from under, which she quickly tucked down the side of her bag.

When Esi got to the school, football practice was on at full tilt again. More bags had been thrown to the side of the playground and people were working in fours and fives, ignoring Lee who was shouting for balls on his head all the time. But Esi's eyes, looking round trying to see all ways at once, weren't for Lee and they weren't for the football. They weren't for Nicky, either, or David or Kompel or Sandra or Kenny, or for any of the others. They were for Kenny's best friend, who wasn't about, however hard she looked.

She stood on the grass and put her bag down slowly, stayed bending for longer than was needed. Wasn't it always the same when you came looking different? It was all hard to keep a straight face while you said your first hello. And she *was* looking different: specially different: she was wearing her headscarf now and it changed the whole look of her. Today she wasn't a Lancashire girl, she was a princess from Ghana. She'd pulled it out of her bag when she was clear of the house and now she was as different and as special as the day she'd first worn it for real.

As she got up from her crouch she heard Kenny shouting and she saw him looking past her towards the school gate. 'Jordan! Come on, pal, you an' me in midfield!'

Esi took her time and turned round slowly to

face the gate while Jordan came along the school path and across the front edge of the playground. He was coming her way, would be passing her to face the gate while Jordan came along the school path and across the front edge of the playground. He was coming her way, would be passing her to get to Kenny and the practice. She stood Ashanti tall, smiled, resisted the want to put her hand to her headscarf and pat it. Well, he'd asked her to wear it, that gave her all the confidence she needed. He'd had his arm round her, he'd held her hand, she had kissed him on the cheek – and he had said how great she'd look if she wore her headscarf today. For him she had taken a great chance, but it was worth it, now that he was here to appreciate it. She watched him as he walked. He hadn't started running when Kenny had shouted, he wasn't rushing to be at the practice; he was walking very special, towards her . . .

She took a small shuffle forward, could see the old Jordan twinkle of his eye. 'Pos-it-i . . .' she started to say to him – as he walked on past.

'What's this? This the team?' he was asking Kenny. He kicked at a loose ball, which went bouncing past Sandra in the goal: and before Esi could get the smile removed from her face, the boy was running and kicking in the practice game.

She turned away, looked nowhere, took a moment. He didn't want the others to know, was that it? He'd been on his own with her last afternoon, hadn't he: when he'd cuddled her, pulled her up, when he'd said something nice outside her house? She turned back and checked him. Yes, she could see that now, it made sense not to make a big show, he wasn't that sort, Jordan. There were private things and there were public things, and he wanted it kept a secret how much he liked her in her headscarf.

She did a couple of skips on the spot, pretended she was warming up, and then she ran and joined in, too, got herself next to Kompel. And in the ten minutes left before school there were others who liked the headscarf, not the way Jordan would, of course, but she started to feel more herself again, not so much the girl come to school with a new look to her. Which was good: but all the same for that, she didn't play well that morning, nowhere near as well as she could: probably because for most of the time her eye was somewhere off the ball.

CHAPTER NINE

B ack in the classroom football was in the air like the week of the Manchester derby. It was as if everyone were waving a scarf two-handed, with *Barton Wood* woven in. Books were open on the tables, but all the talk was about the long ball or the short, about four-three-three against three-three-four, and about liberos and sweepers, and far posts and near crosses. Everyone was at Maine Road or Old Trafford in their heads – except Mrs Clegg, and Miranda Pudsey, who had at last abandoned houses and was drawing a line-up of dolls for the Nursery: and Esi Mensah, in her headscarf, who was sitting turning the pages of her book while she tried accidentally to catch Jordan's eye.

For a while Mrs Clegg's attention was on totting-up the week's dinner-monies, just throwing out 'Thank you!' and 'Right!' every now and then as if something were about to happen: and it did, when the dinner-book balanced at last. She brought a ruler down on to her desk with a bull-whip crack, like something going off.

'*Thank you!*' And the words which came after were measured out as if they cost a thousand pounds per milligram of breath. 'If . . . I . . . hear . . . another . . . word . . . about . . . this . . . *blessed* . . . football . . . match . . . I . . . shall . . . cancel . . . it.' She let that sink in. 'It is within my gift to do so.'

No one was sure what that meant. She hadn't come in with anything wrapped, but the look on her face showed a dislike of football which ought not to be tested.

'Is it tomorrow, Miss?' Sandra Smith, as usual, said something without troubling a brain cell.

'Shut up, Sandra!'

'Stupid Smith!'

Other messages also reached Sandra: not so much words as clenched fists and twisted faces.

'Is *what* tomorrow?' Mrs Clegg seemed as if all she wanted now was just one more word from someone to get her covering their pitch with a metre of ice.

Sandra tried to find some way out but couldn't. Her mouth was like the Mersey Tunnel. There was a long and painful staring.

'Burying the chest again, Miss. Tomorrow? Is it true they dug up the treasure chest again? Mrs Clegg?' Kompel tried distraction. 'Someone said they dug it up.'

'Yeah, Miss, Friday night.' Kenny was in quick. And others weighed in fast about the digging up of the chest; but not Esi – and not, Esi was pleased to see, Jordan, who knew . . .

Mrs Clegg was waving a hand in the air like a referee disallowing a penalty call. 'Don't ask me. I'm not here in the afternoons. What happens in the afternoons is a closed book to me.'

'Yeah, it is to me, an' all.' Lee Rayner couldn't resist. 'An' the mornings!'

'Something they forgot, no sweat.' Jordan had decided to speak, in case Rayner's mouth might get Mrs Clegg's gift dished out.

'What got forgot?' Kompel wanted to know.

'Something,' Jordan shrugged – and as he took a look across at Esi he got a winner of a nice smile back.

In all of which the heat was going off the football, and Mrs Clegg's attention was coming on to Jordan.

'And what have you forgotten?' She flicked her earlobe with a finger. 'It's PE today. You shouldn't be wearing an earring, Jordan Jenkins. Take it out.'

Jordan knew the rules. You hadn't to wear anything in PE lessons which could hurt yourself or pull a partner's hair or strangle them. So earrings and bracelets and dangling dummies were out on PE days, when they weren't allowed to be worn for the lesson. He did as he was told, opened the earring and hooked it out of his lobe: but as he stood up to go to put it in the valuable box, Mrs Sherry came in carrying the plastic picnic hamper from the treasure chest – and wearing that special News Flash look headteachers use on Infants.

'That's it! What I said . . .' Kompel started.

'That the same box?' David asked.

And Sandra fell off her chair patting Kompel on the back for being right.

'This is just in case you've heard rumours and you think there's anything secret going on,' Mrs Sherry told them. 'Something got put in by mistake: but we're going to put this back at playtime, bury it under the tree again.' She held up her hand against any more questions. 'But see what great good fortune we've had! Look what came in today's post!' From her pocket she pulled a brown envelope.

'Child benefit!' Lee guessed. To which he got the benefit of a Sherry freeze.

'If this had come on Friday it would certainly have gone in with the valuables.' She spent a few seconds making the most of getting out the envelope's contents, in the end holding up a postcard to which had been Sellotaped a small, circular, dull brownish-black object. 'It's from the farmer who used to own this land. It's a Roman coin with the head of Augustus Caesar upon it, dug up by the farmer's plough in the nineteen thirties. Isn't that marvellous?'

'I think I'm gonna faint!' Nicky told Lee.

'So after a little look, in it goes, with the valuables. A part of the history of Barton Wood.' Mrs Sherry handed the postcard round, some holding it with wonder, passing it on as if Barton Wood's past might crumble in their hands, others getting rid like Beat Your Neighbour. When they'd finished she put it in the top of the plastic picnic valuables box she had come in with, which was now sitting on the teachers' desk. 'You can look at it till playtime.'

Nicky crossed his eyes. But Kompel was impressed. 'That means, when this goes down there's going to be real buried treasure under Barton Wood.'

'Indeed. Lucky, wasn't it, Esi?' Mrs Sherry winked at the headscarf girl. 'And isn't that pretty?' she said, touching the African material as she went.

Which was an attention to the headscarf Esi would have liked from Jordan; but in the classroom from Mrs Sherry it was embarrassing, and worse. It was illegal.

'Esi Mensah, I don't know what you're wearing that for.' It was as if Mrs Clegg tried deliberately to undo the things Mrs Sherry did. 'It's PE – that could catch on the wallbars and strangle you. Take it off.'

Esi put her hand to her headscarf, held it there until the light in the teacher's eyes had started shining elsewhere, when she put it down again.

'Now, we've wasted enough of our hall time. So, shorts, T-shirts, shoes untied for slipping off in the hall. Jordan, earring . . .' From her desk drawer Mrs Clegg took the large cigar box she used for watches and such items. 'Come on, bracelets, watches, rings . . .'

They were ready fast. The girls turned their backs and clamped clothing under their chins while they did a quick change; the boys had mostly come to school ready. Watches and rings and valuable odds and ends were put in the cigar box, and then the sitting up straight was a model of superb behaviour, just waiting for Sandra to stop taking all day unstrapping her Mickey Mouse watch: no one liked wasting P E time.

Except Miranda Pudsey. She had been quietly felt-tipping her picture through everything, not thumping anyone, not calling anyone names and not starting stupid arguments. A few looked round to her to see if she was going to hold them up; but they saw Mrs Clegg looking, too, and by looking away again deciding to let peace reign. Miranda could do her own thing.

But not Esi Mensah. 'And that scarf thing, please.'

'Please, Mrs Clegg, it's precious . . .'

'Then it shouldn't have come to school.' The woman was looking at her watch, and the rest were throwing daggers. Another second and Clegg would cancel P E altogether. Only Sandra was lingering for a private view of the Roman coin in the treasure box. Esi took off her headscarf. She looked at Jordan for some pity, but he was sitting up all teacher's pet.

'Fold it and put it with the valuables.'

Esi folded it small. The bright material wasn't thick; it was the same as the dress, meant to be worn in the African sun. And she really felt stupid now, it was all so out of place: all right in a photo, or at a christening, but Barton Wood was never Kumasi — so why had she gone all Independence Day for stupid Jordan? She came out of her seat to go to the desk, but Mrs Clegg was clicking fingers at her.

'No, don't you . . . Give it to Sandra. Sandra, box, please.' Sandra was nearer. Esi gave the thing to Sandra as Mrs Clegg commanded. 'Right, door!' and there was the usual rush to line up.

An elbow put Esi behind Jordan. She stared into the back of his neck and he looked round: she found herself smiling when she should have pulled a face. 'Did you see it? She made me take it off. Wore it special.' She hated herself every so often, Esi.

'What's that?'

She pushed him in the back. What else to do with the stupid dilk? It was as if he'd been some other person on Friday. What was it with him?

She looked at him in PE and she looked at them all, rushing round and round the cacao-trees, as her mother said, pushing each other about and having to be either first or last. What was it with boys? Why couldn't they ever behave any older than Seth? She climbed to the top of a rope. Why were they such big let-downs?

The rest of the day was no better. She did her best not to show any interest in Mr Dunphy and Mr Higgins burying the chest again, just in case people started asking questions, and she went to the meeting for the football team because everyone her age had to be there – there were only just enough for a proper team in the whole school – but she sat by the door and she kept herself quiet. There was an argument at dinner-time between Lee Rayner and David Kent about who was the best footballer – typical – and she kept herself out of that as well. The day had lost its shine, no way round that; hadn't begun to live up to her hopes for it. The afternoon was a bit brighter – the afternoons always were, because Mrs Sherry taught them, and she always read them a good story.

At twenty to three Mrs Sherry shut the book to the usual Aaahs! 'Now then, jobs to do before last play.' She gave out various tidying things. 'Have you all got your watches and rings from the valuables box?'

It was only Jordan, with his earring, who hadn't, and Esi, who had left her wasted headscarf off and in its safe place till home time. They went up together to get their things while the rest of the room sorted trays and had reading books checked out; put pencils back in the pencil-pots and paint-brushes in the scissors rack; and while all the usual talk went on.

'Miss, did it all get buried back? That Roman coin and everything?'

'It did, thanks to the kindness of Mr Dunphy.'

Esi kept her eyes on the lid of the valuables box.

'Did he bury Pudsey with it?'

'That's nasty, Nicky – and her name's Miranda.'

'Only, she's not here, Miss. Is she?'

Mrs Sherry looked around. 'No she isn't.' She called to Kompel. 'Go to Mrs Swainsgate, will you? Ask her to come along . . .'

None of this – suddenly – was of any interest to Esi. Jordan was fixing his earring and having a look round the class before getting over to Kenny: but that wasn't what was holding Esi at the desk: nothing to do with Jordan. What had her staring at the cigar box empty of valuables was that it was just that: empty. Everyone had got their rings and watches out; and the only thing left had been Jordan's earring. Which meant her headscarf was somewhere else. But where? She left the desk and bumped through the tidying to get to Mrs Sherry.

'Miss, have you seen it? My headscarf? It was folded small, what I wore in my picture, what you said was pretty . . .'

'No. Where was it? Where did you put it?' But the way she was staring over heads to the door, her real worry was out of the room, was Miranda.

'In the valuables box. Mrs Clegg said.'

'Then it must be in there, mustn't it?'

'But it's not, Miss.'

When Mrs Sherry started to run out of patience things were on their way to being serious; but the noise the rest were making was getting out of hand. She clapped her hands and called for quiet. 'Then are you sure you put it there?'

'No, Miss, Sandra did.'

'Ask Sandra, then.' The headteacher was going round the room saying things to different people instead of having a good shout, but she was really on the wait for Mrs Swainsgate. Trailing Esi behind her, she had a quick word with Sandra.

'I put it in . . . a . . . valuables box, Miss.'

'*A* valuables box? I don't think I understand.'

But Esi did. Even as Mrs Swainsgate came in to be asked to go and look round the lavatories and the classrooms for Miranda Pudsey – and to telephone home if she thought she'd run off – and as Mrs Sherry's concentration went well off the headscarf, Esi knew what Sandra Smith meant.

A valuables box.

There had been two boxes of valuables on Mrs Clegg's desk. The cigar box for PE valuables: and the time capsule valuables box, for burying again with the Roman coin inside. And Sandra Smith, being Sandra Stupid Smith, had put her precious only-one-in-the-world headscarf in the box that had been buried. Having been dug up for Esi Mensah once already.

And Sandra knew. As she led her out to play crying, she had her arm round the girl like at a funeral, told the others as they went how she'd thought – the headscarf being so special – that that was what they'd wanted: to bury it. A bit of Somewhere Else in Barton Wood.

'Somewhere Else?'

'Africa. Where it come from . . .'

'Was it Esi's stuff they had to dig up before?' Kompel Vasisht had read all the looks, wasn't stupid.

'It went . . . with the dress.' Esi was doing more sobbing than talking these days. 'It's . . . special.'

David Kent came across the playground from telling Lee Rayner where to put his captain's armband – round his big mouth. Kompel told him Esi's troubles. 'It's in the chest for a hundred years . . .'

David listened. He was the sort who did listen, head held just at a tilt, which had other people listening, too.

'Can't you cut a bit off the bottom, stick that round your head?' Jordan suggested.

Esi gave him no time of day for that: the kid who hadn't even looked at it! There wasn't hem enough, anyhow.

'Tell Mrs Sherry,' David concluded. 'She'll have to do something about it.'

'No, they'll never dig it up again.' Kenny wasn't sparing feelings by mincing up the truth. 'They'll say, "Tough, pal!" and write a little letter to your mum.'

Sandra said she'd get her mum to look round the market, but she knew that was daft before she'd started saying it: Pennington Market wasn't anywhere near Somewhere Else.

In the end, sympathetic as people may be, try as they might to cheer you up and make suggestions and share your tissues crying – it's you on your own in the end. Losing something precious is a solo business, and it was only Esi who was going to have to go home without her Ghanaian headscarf.

'I don't know what I'm going to do!' she wailed, and she crumpled down so flat to the ground that no one's arms could reach low enough to get round her.

CHAPTER TEN

They found Miranda in the Nursery. At three o'clock coats were being done up and damp paintings being given to child-minders and parents; it was all toggles and żips and Velcro, and toys being forced out of tight little hands; the usual end of day traffic jam with push-chairs coming in through the playground door and Mrs Sherry getting knee-height cuddles as she came in from the corridor. Talking to three people at once, the Nursery teacher nodded her over to the Home Corner. Mrs Sherry tiptoed to the little house. It was all shut up – the small door, the window, the checkered curtains. She fingered a curtain to one side.

Miranda was sitting doing a chalk-board picture for little Carl, talking him through the violent drawing. 'See? There's his big gun, an' that's the pile of bodies, and there's all the blood, all over the floor . . .' The boy's eyes were big, and he pushed Miranda's hand to go on scribbling the red as she saw Mrs Sherry peeping through the curtains. 'An' he saw this big giant and he wanted to know if he needed sortin' an' all . . .' With a wipe of her sleeve she smeared the picture off. 'Now I'll do you an ugly monster!'

Mrs Sherry went back to the Nursery teacher. 'How long's she been here?' She tied a shoe stuck up at her.

'All the afternoon, good as gold. I thought you'd sent her.'

Mrs Sherry shook her head. 'I'd send a note, love.'

'Well, she's been a good little pair of hands. Loves it with the babies . . .'

'Watch it! She might do you out of a job!' Mrs Sherry went back to the Home Corner. 'Come on, Miranda, time to tidy up before home.'

And, still good as gold, Miranda went.

'I've been very worried about you.'

'It's nice in here. They kiss you.'

'Come on.' She put an arm round the girl, and kept it there till they were both back at the class-room door.

If Esi had reckoned she was on her own she had reckoned wrong. None of her friends ran off straight home; David and Kompel took her to a quiet place near the the small wooden bridge, where Jordan was waiting, and Kenny, and Sandra.

'They dug it up before, only had to ask them,' Jordan told her. 'Old Jordan soon sorted it, eh?'

'So, you fancy asking them again?'

Old Jordan wasn't so sure about that. Besides

which, the teachers would all be shooting off home, wouldn't they?

Chins were rubbed.

'Why'd you want to wear it, if it was that marvellous and valuable?' he asked.

Esi tried to hit him. 'Because you liked it, Jordan Jenkins: you told me to wear it, didn't you?'

Which left him muttering something about heads and gas ovens, and staring out the stares.

'My grandad's got a spade,' Kenny offered.

'Can't you say it got lost in the move?' Sandra was already skipping round the bridge. 'I lost tons of things. They lost my bed, I had to sleep in the bath.'

'In the water?'

'No, stupid!'

'That's where they'll put my body!' Esi stood in the way of the skipping. 'When my mum's finished killing me, my dad'll start killing me all over again. I got to wear that dress . . .'

They all looked about them as if there were clues stuck around like at a party: over the bridge, up in the sky, down on the ground, in the bushes: on each other's foreheads.

'Right, Es!' David took charge. 'Cross your fingers they don't want to see it before tonight . . .'

Esi frowned at him.

'Because tonight – Kenny's right – us, we're just going to dig it up ourselves!'

'Yeah!' Jordan exploded.

And even after a bit of thought, it really was the only answer.

'Right!' Kompel pointed at Kenny. 'You bring your grandad's spade.'

And Sandra was jumping up and down. 'And I'll bring . . . what shall I bring?'

'You bring yourself,' David told her. 'And I'll see you lot, six o'clock, here. Dunphy'll be having his tea, or over the pub.' He had a sudden doubt. 'Can you get out?' he asked Esi.

Esi hadn't thought of that.

'She'll get out,' Jordan told them. 'I'll sort that. Pos–it–ive!'

And Esi believed in him again.

With good cause, as it turned out. At ten to six he was ringing at her front doorbell – and being answered by Mrs Mensah and a shining in the face from Seth's torch.

'Where was you, Esi?' He squinted up his eyes to where she was flittering behind them. 'Football practice! Come on!'

'Eh? What's this?' Mrs Mensah had that don't-forget-I'm-standing-here face on her.

'Sorry. Forgot to tell you.' Esi stayed the blind side of her mother for the lying.

'Forgot? Our number six an' she forgets!' Jordan asked the bricks round the front door for their opinion of that. 'We won't win St Paul's tomorrow 'less we're all there.'

Mrs Mensah twisted both ways to finally get a look at her daughter. 'All where? What's going on, girl?'

'Our school. We're playing this other school, and I'm in it.'

'In it?' Jordan was in danger of going a note or two too high: and Mrs Mensah was not of the easily taken-in breed of mother. 'She's only vital!'

But as Esi grabbed her coat, it looked like Mrs Mensah was operating on some other wavelength: no suspicions about a headscarf, she knew nothing of that, and not the truth of the football at all, but the going out with a boy: you could see it in the tilt of her head.

'Where you going?' she wanted to know.

'Only over the school,' Jordan told her. A clear conscience there.

'Then don't you be late! School's all right – but one hour, top load, or I'll be over looking for you!'

Esi squeezed past Seth, closed her eyes to a torch beam like a lie-detector, and confided in her mother, 'Told him I needed practice!' Girl to girl.

And with a years-back look in her eye, Mrs Mensah watched the pair of them go down to the garden gate.

'What the dickens do you want my spade for? Don't tell me you're going to start digging the garden?'

The look in Kenny's grandad's eye was definitely one of suspicion. Kenny was in the garden shed trying to make off with the spade – but the old man had come out of the house at the rattle of tools and was in the shed doorway standing between Kenny and the garden path, an arm leaned casually across the opening. And Kenny wasn't a Jordan who could come up with some quick line to get out on.

'I just want it for something.'

'Good news, the dog does enough digging up round here: I'm thinking of getting him an allotment.'

'It's just a job I've got to do.'

His grandad looked at him, one of those stares which normally went with a clucking of his tongue. 'Come on, what you up to, Kenny?'

And then inspiration came; a little piece of buried truth. 'Digging up a Roman coin. Yeah, Julius Caesar. This farmer found this old five pence near our school . . .'

'Oh, an architectural dig.' Kenny still couldn't tell when his grandad was serious and when he wasn't. 'Your teacher involved in it, is she?'

But direct lies were out. 'It's in the school field,' he nodded.

'So we might go to bed rich?'

Kenny shrugged. He wouldn't want to seem that hopeful.

'Yeah, I doubt it, an' all, our Kenny. I doubt a lot about it . . .' And Grandad Bayfield let up his arm like a car-park barrier. 'But don't be late – and don't lose that spade or you'll be digging my spuds with your bare hands.'

By which time Kenny was at the side gate.

'Reckon I was born on a winkle barge?' the old man called after him.

★

David led them in a single file around the edge of the school field. They had squeezed through a tear in the chain-link fencing and were creeping round like Mohicans, would probably have stood out less if they'd wandered aimless in a gang and pretended someone had moved the street corner. Kompel was there, and Esi and Jordan and Kenny with the spade. And Sandra – who'd run to catch them up wearing a knitted Balaclava with just her eyes showing. 'Hello!' she'd said, putting on a deep voice.

'Wotcha, Sandra.' Jordan wasn't playing any daft games tonight.

'Fooled my mum!' She'd taken off the hot hat with a scratch.

Now they were coming to a clump of shrubs not far from where the chest had been buried, everyone pumped up with the buzz of doing some wicked thing for a very good cause. Their hearts were going, and their faces had those tight looks which weren't far off small smiles. They'd cop it for trespass and all sorts it they got caught, could be 'attempted robbery' as well. And the danger of an upset was not the other side of the moon. Around at the other side of the school, Patrick Dunphy was coming out of the pub. He had had his drink, sitting up at the bar like the squire off the next door estate, and now he was taking a short cut across the school grounds to his supper. From out of his pocket he pulled his latest computer game, which bleeped at him as if he were an android. Esi and the others hadn't seen him, and the bleeps weren't carrying that far: and they were too busy, anyway, skinning their eyes in the fading light for the right place to dig.

'Here it is, where it's dead.' Sandra was on her hands and knees.

The others looked, and they went with the nods from Jordan and Esi, who had been there once before. 'Get the turfs up carefully,' David instructed. 'Lay them over there in the same order they come up.' He began cutting into the flattened grass with an upright spade, all eyes on the job in hand, Esi visualizing that headscarf coming out of the box, feeling its thin length wound around her hand as she went to take it home.

Bleep-bleep.

'Struth!' David looked up. 'Hit the ground!'

He threw himself flat and down went Esi and Kenny and Jordan and Kompel. Only Sandra started patting the grass – until a boot on the backside flattened her as well.

For Kenny it was like that first day when he'd been watching the school going up, the day he'd had to get the ball back. Then he'd been down in the cold grass looking through these short stalks.

Bleep-bleep.

'It's Dunphy!'

'Still coming!'

'Going home. Past here!'

And Esi shivered in the dew. For her the dread of him finding them was real, and likely.

Patrick Dunphy knew his way through the

school; once he was across the playground where a little wall might have tripped him, it was open grass to the small gate on the far side, so he could play with his game as he went. And he needed to: he had just given a man a few quid for this in the pub, and he wanted to be sure he'd got full value before the bloke went home.

Bleep-bleep.

'Oooer . . .'

For a second it was as if Dunphy thought the noise was from the game in his hand; but he looked up, and there she was. Someone in a woollen helmet, coming at him like a sleep-walker.

'I'm lost. I've lost my way,' said this deep unbroken voice.

'What you doing in here, young Sandra?'

'Where am I?'

'You've no more lost your way than I have, cutting through, I know you.' He switched off his game and put it in his top. 'Come on, you live by me, I'm escorting you out; you can go round by the road.' And putting time on his own journey to be the diligent caretaker, he led her back to the school entrance and made her go round by the road, walking with her and ticking her off for trespassing, all the way home.

The diggers did a quick and quiet fist clench in the air before the spade was cutting down into the soil again. The earth was loose, and once below the first thirty centimetres the dig went faster – Kenny at his grandad's spade and Esi diving in and out to look.

'There it is! I can see it!' She was on her knees and clawing with her fingers.

They threw the spade aside and everyone got down to the soil, earth under their fingernails like Gardening Club gone mad.

'Come on, let's have it out.' David had a hand beneath a corner of the box; which was more reluctant to come at the end than anyone had reckoned. But with a last heave, which had Kompel over, they got it up and on to the grass.

'Yes! Got a result!' Jordan crowed.

'Sandra lost it, Sandra made sure we found it!' Esi was crying with relief and with pleasure: and, Sandra not being there for the thanking, she kissed Jordan on the cheek again. 'Pos-it-ive!' she said.

'Pos-it-ive!' David had the box open. 'Here we go!'

'End of all your troubles!' said Kenny.

'Sleep again now, Esi!' Kompel gave the happy girl a hug.

David had the lid off and they all looked in. And there it all was, all the special items they'd put in to show what the 1990s were about, and on the top the Roman coin Sellotaped to the school postcard.

But they couldn't see any headscarf. Not on top, not down the side, not underneath.

No one said a thing at first. They had every item out of the treasure chest, careful to start with but ending up scrabbling through photographs and data sheets and bits and pieces till the box looked like a desecrated coffin.

But the headscarf was not there.

'It's not there,' Esi said, simply, quietly, no tears and no wobble in her voice; just matter-of-fact like the telling of a death.

'Sandra said it was, definitely,' Kompel said, looking around as if the headscarf could have flown up a tree, or into a bush.

'Well, it's not. Is it?' Now Esi did begin to cry, those slow serious tears which come saltier.

Each looked at the others. There was a long silence, just the sounds of a bone crunch in the fierce hug Jordan gave the girl.

'Oh-oh!' he said quietly into her ear. 'Neg-at-ive!'

Kenny was sat up on the kitchen counter, being measured for a pair of shin-pads. Not a pair of Buktas from a Pennington sports shop, but a pair of his grandad's specials made from a *Sunday Mirror* magazine, folded paper Sellotaped thick, with arches cut out for the ankles. And too slow a job for Kenny, who was leg-shaking to get down.

'Come on, Grandad, we've got a practice. They're giving out the positions!'

Never mind last night and the sweat of digging up and burying that chest, today was the day of the match against St Paul's, and already the blood was injected with adrenalin. Montgomery the dog had a fight with a crucial page which Grandad Bayfield just about fooled off him. 'You got to go right, lad. What we do is, we tape this round your leg before kick-off.'

A real twist inside Kenny. *Kick-off!* His impatient leg-shaking became a trembling, not far short of fear. He looked at his gran who was ironing his white shorts.

'What tops you playing in, Kenny? Got a set of school colours, have you? What am I gonna shout? "Come on, you Reds!" or "Away the Blues!"?'

'Dunno. We're borrowing off the other school, whatever they've got to spare.'

'We like to know what we're goin' to shout.' His grandad made neat rolls of the pads for going in the bag.

Gran Bayfield spat on her iron. 'You remember you're at a school, not on no terraces!'

'You really coming to see me play?'

'You keep us away! Weren't a game of your dad's we never saw.' Grandad Bayfield ruffled the dog. 'Eh, Montgomery?' The old man looked up, just for a moment his eyes like he'd been out in the wind. 'Never thought this'd come so quick, pal.'

Gran thumped her iron hard on the turn of a hem. 'Stop crying and drink your gin! The boy's growing up.' She folded the shorts into Kenny's sports bag while Grandad stood back to give Kenny room to jump down.

Grandad cuffed his nose. 'Yeah. We'll see you 'safternoon, lad, give Montgomery his walk. An' you use your small size, spin on a sixpence like I used to do. Some of them big fellows need Spaghetti Junction to turn round.'

Kenny shoved his makeshift shin-pads in on top of his gear. His dad and his grandad had spent nights going over all the professional tricks, all the things the short and the nippy could do if they had any skill at all: and up to this morning it had been exciting and matey, but nicely far off, future stuff. Now today was the day – on a real pitch with marked lines and goal-posts up instead of coats; with people watching from both the schools. In Kenny's head a grandstand had suddenly grown along the side of the field, and a certain roaring filled his ears, though it could have been the sound of his own blood.

Grandad ruffled the boy's head as if he were the dog. 'Good luck, pal. You show 'em, for all the Bayfields and the Holbrooks, eh?'

The Holbrooks. His mum's old name. 'Yeah. Ta-ra.' He scooped up his bag and got out through the back door before any more could be said, ran round the house to the front.

In the kitchen, Gran Bayfield took a while putting down the ironing-board. 'What wouldn't I give for her to have seen him today?' She looked across at her husband.

But he couldn't look her back. He shut the door Kenny had left ajar, and with his eyes to the floor he suddenly did something rare. He came across and put his arm round the woman, gave her a squeeze. 'Come on, lass. P'raps she's watching, eh?'

It being the day of the football match was at the very bottom of Esi's pile of worries. Yesterday she'd lost her headscarf, and it hadn't been in the only likely place. Now she had her special dress out of the wardrobe while she did a double check on the hem. She'd dreamed all night of it being nice and wide after all and she'd woken up that morning with her problem all solved: a little bit of needlework from someone like Kompel's mum and no one would ever know. She'd actually smiled to herself – before she'd opened her eyes and realized where she was – in her new Barton Wood bedroom, and not the old room of her dreams: back to real life with a quick sick pain, and no problem solved at all. It was as plain and cold as the new light of day: the hem of the dress as it lay on the bed was no more than two centimetres wide, you'd fight to get a ribbon out of it. Now she couldn't wait to get to school to turn her classroom upside down.

But no chance till after Assembly, first thing: and what Sandra met her with as they lined up to go into the hall was, 'Got your head thing, Es?' There were times when she asked for a right face-pulling at her. She had to be told about the treasure chest blank. 'Glad I'm not you!' she said with a comforting smile.

'Wish I wasn't anyone!' Miranda threw in, for nothing.

And Esi could understand Miranda a bit. 'Me an' all,' she said.

In Assembly the theme was the football match, starting earlier than planned in the singing of *Kumbaya*.

'*Let us win, my Lord, let us win . . .*' Jordan sang.
'*Million nil, my Lord, a million nil . . .*'
'Every day is a red-letter day for Barton Wood,' Mrs Sherry told them as they sat cross-legged in

their lines. 'And today we're going on to our field to play a football match.' It was as if she'd seen too many Shakespeare films.

Kenny sat up, Esi slumped down. Mr Higgins smiled along at his squad as if he were pleased it was official now, mentioned in the hall.

'But for me, and for Mr Higgins, the important thing is that we play a fair game, and that we enjoy it. Win, lose or draw, we enjoy it. It's not the winning or the losing, it's how we play the game.'

'Hard!' said Lee to the people around him. 'Play hard!'

'So let's all go forward and have a good day . . .'

'Go forward and get a good hard result!'

'Yeah!'

Kenny looked along at the proud line of players, everyone with Wembley in their eyes – except Esi, who seemed to have the bottomless pit. Now he was at school sitting next to Jordan the worst of his nerves had gone and his body had started tingling with the feel of a pleasure he'd forgotten: looking forward to something – to a birthday, or Christmas, or an outing: the first looking forward he'd done since his mum had died. Never mind that aggro with the ball, never mind that horror in the cupboard with Miranda Pudsey, never mind being small: today he was in the Barton Wood squad, and they were all in together, all going forward for a good result – in front of their parents, and him in front of Gran and Grandad and Montgomery. He sucked in a proud breath and counted them off: Jordan and Lee and Nicky and David and –

He almost ricked his neck checking the line again. *David? David Kent?* He poked Jordan as they all stood up. Where the heck was David Kent?

'Where's Kenty?'

Jordan looked about as they all moved forward. He shrugged. Kenny asked Esi, who didn't hear him. He asked Lee, who didn't care. But Kenny cared — David Kent was vital, he was the best player they'd got, of his bigger type. It took the edge off everything if he wasn't there.

'We can't play without David Kent!'

So where the devil was he?

He was waiting by his mother's car, which was still parked in their driveway, miserably bouncing a football picked up from the new turf at the front of their house — and not letting the dew on to his jumper on pain of a roasting when she came out.

Their house was on a corner, one of the larger 'executive' properties which had had special treatment because David's father had bribed for it. Where others on the estate were waiting for their kitchens to be fitted, the Kents' was being redone to a better standard. Where the other fronts were still waiting for the Rotavator, the Kents' was laid bowling-green perfect, and where other drives were waiting for asphalt, the Kents' was laid with herring-bone bricks. David's father treated trades-people like servants, and somehow it seemed to work for him.

Trish Kent came out of the house: and it had to

be said that David was proud of her when he saw her looking like this. She was a beautiful woman – a fashion model who'd only just given up – the sort who had drivers' heads on back to front when she motored past them. She was a bit like Kompel was when she stood up proud, white instead of Asian, but with that something inside which seemed to shine out.

And he'd have liked to throw the football at her beautiful head as she came out of their white and brass door: her silk blouse showing smooth neck and no jewellery as she leaned to the Volvo and unlocked it, went to slide herself on to the seat.

'It's our football match today! Who wants going to some other school?'

They'd had it out indoors, three times since his father's bomb had gone off the night before, and still David couldn't see it. His father had talked a lot of guff about *Grant Maintained* and *Voluntary* which he hadn't understood, before a new bottle of something strong had got opened and he'd said he didn't want to hear any more buts about it. And at bedtime his mother had only parroted all the same talk, as if she didn't really believe in it herself: so she was the one to go for.

'It's because my pals are ordinary kids, live up the road, that's it, isn't it?'

'Is that what you think?' She came out of the car to give the windscreen a long-fingered wipe with a tissue. 'I was an ordinary child, I lived an ordinary sort of life.' Which was true: you could hear the north in her voice. 'And don't say "kids", say "children" or "pupils" – "kids" are animals.'

So that was it, it *was* the friends he had, because they all said kids.

'Come on, get in, we do have an appointment.'

In a quick kick of temper the ball went somewhere he didn't care. He got into the car, shut the door and sat uncomfortable on the soft leather seat in the back, because she wouldn't have a son his age showing up the front.

And the worst of it was, as he already knew, the school they were driving to was the rival, St Paul's Church of England in the old village on the other side of the canal: the school Barton Wood would be playing at football that afternoon. With him on the wrong line, like someone transferred, and not knowing what to shout.

At Barton Wood they were carrying on without him: morning play and a training session, with all the skills being coached. Mr Higgins was showing Sandra how to catch a ball to her stomach and hold it there, with an off-target Esi throwing the balls. Mr Dunphy the caretaker was showing Kompel and Kenny how to mark up against a Nicky and Lee coming at them; while Sandra's brother Billy and Jordan and others were running up and down the hall passing balls with the insides of their feet. But the team was definitely short of David Kent, and while there were plenty of younger children who could be in the squad, Barton Wood really did need some size.

Kompel went to the toilet, saw Miranda feeding the pets in the patio area: well, even Miranda looked of a size, sitting there cuddling a heavy white rabbit. 'Oh, she loves you, doesn't she; she looks right comfy.' Kompel got a stare at her intrusion. 'We're short for football, you want being in?'

Miranda shook her head, a sharp double shake.

'No sweat, Miranda, I'm asking everyone.'

Miranda put her head to the rabbit, stroked it again. 'Waste of time, innit, girl? Better things to kick than footballs, in't there?'

Kompel backed off. It had been stupid asking: but not half as stupid as trying to play St Paul's without David Kent to keep everything calm.

Bob Guest, the head of St Paul's, had left the pumping of practice balls to keep his appointment with the Kents. Thick dark hair, a shiny chin, and giving off the air of someone who would sooner be out on the field, he sat in his track suit in front of the trophy cabinet in his study, looking more like a successful manager being interviewed for *The Big Match* than the head of a Church of England primary school. Opposite him, Trish Kent was seated very elegant, no problems for her with low arm-chairs and short skirts. David, edging it on an upright, had just now been further depressed at the lines of the enemy who'd passed him as he waited in the corridor outside; but he was suddenly seeing more hopeful specks in the sunlight.

'I'm sorry, Mrs Kent, I just haven't got room. We're like the fat man and the bath, we're full to overflowing.'

'Oh, surely . . .' David's mother said. She leaned forward slightly.

'That's a fact. Too many kids.'

She sat back again.

'I'm just going to have to ask you to be patient, play the waiting game.' Mr Guest folded his arms as if for a team photograph. 'You've seen round the school and I'm glad you like it – but we have to abide by standard numbers.' Mr Guest winked comfortingly; not normally a winking man. 'I'll give you word as soon as there's any sign of movement . . .'

But if David thought that was that for the time being, that things could go back to being simple for a while longer, he was turned round on himself when he got out to the corridor again. The school was in the original 1877 building, as different in design to Barton Wood as a cuckoo clock to Lego: dark where Barton Wood was light, gloomy where the other was colourful, narrow where the new school was wide, awkward steps where Barton Wood was on the level: and where every area in Barton Wood opened out to several other places, here the corridor was narrow and straight, and led only to the front door. Through which, who was coming but Mr Higgins from Barton Wood – looking over kids' heads going out to play to wave at Mr Guest. And David knew what the man wanted. He'd come for the football strip – the colours David was supposed to be playing in.

David's mother didn't know Mr Higgins; what was more important, he didn't know who she was; but he'd know David when he saw him all right – the player who hadn't said he wouldn't show up today. And he felt badly enough about that as it was, without being seen in this opponent school. Desperately, he looked around as Mr Higgins sorted his feet out from a mat-well. But, no hope, there was no place for ducking out of sight: and his stupid mother was making herself taller at the sight of someone coming, and slimmer: there was no tucking himself in behind her, either.

David looked around again, tried to think of something to say. But what was there? *Good luck! Hope you win!*? 'Struth! What a downer, what a pits day: his father's bomb-blast of a decision, and then just as he'd been let off the hook, here he was looking the traitor for Higgins!

He was almost bumped full into view there and then by two tall girls coming along with the flow, carrying several hangers of Elizabethan costumes. He'd seen them before, waiting to go in, he'd had a smile off one. Now he got another. And suddenly finding himself doing it before he'd even thought he'd had the thought, he took a costume off the first, held it up in front of his face. 'Want a hand with that?'

And while Mr Guest must have reckoned how polite he was, he helped the girls with the costumes past Mr Higgins, gave them back with a smile, and waited for his mother outside the front door.

The lesson going on for the top class was to find strong structures around the school: the triangles made by the caretaker's ladder, the shape of chair legs and the support of the roof. But Esi was on her own activity; no strong structure on her list of wants, just a weak width of printed cotton which had no practical use at all: a decorative headscarf, but the only one of its kind in the whole of the country. And, good mate that she was, Kompel had done her own work just enough to get by, and was helping her in her looking: not too official, because the last thing Esi wanted was that letter – or a phone call – going home. Pretending to be still sorting strong shapes from weak, Kompel with a sheet of paper and Esi with a pencil, they looked under cupboards and on them, felt beneath heaters and behind them, lifted carpets and scattered cushions, rummaged in today's bins and even delved out in the yard in yesterday's sacks of rubbish. But wherever they searched, whatever new place they started running to, the headscarf was not to be found. It hadn't been in the chest last night, and now it wasn't in the classroom and it wasn't in the rubbish. But it wasn't any use to anyone, just a scrap to a stranger: and there was no one with a grudge on Esi to make them want to hide it or destroy it. Was there?

'Esi?' Mrs Sherry had come outside to them. 'Kompel?'

Esi looked at the headteacher's face, at the hands behind her back; she didn't look happy and she didn't look sad, but she definitely didn't look as if she'd found something. Had it turned up? It was people with nothing faces on who sometimes told you the important things. Esi didn't dare blink.

'What are you doing here?'

'Looking for strong shapes, Miss.' Kompel took a great interest in an angle-iron to the waste-sack support.

'And just in case we see my headscarf . . .'

'Ah. Haven't you found that?'

A shaking of heads.

'Oh, Lord!' Mrs Sherry put her hand to her mouth. 'It couldn't, could it? Not a second time? I mean,' she dropped her voice, 'the valuables box and . . . the treasure chest valuables box . . .?'

'No, Miss, definitely.' Said perhaps a bit too quickly.

Mrs Sherry gave Esi a look. 'With Sandra? How can you be so sure?'

Kompel came round from behind the headteacher. 'Don't they say lightning don't strike twice?' she asked. 'Something like that?'

'They do: but it does – and I just wonder how you can be so sure. You know, I think I'd be pleading to have that treasure chest dug up again . . .'

'No, definitely. I just know . . .'

'Well, it won't be any further down in that rubbish – and make sure you wash your hands:

then go round the rooms.' Mrs Sherry gave them a long look, and walked on to the Nursery, through its small fenced play area with the high bolted gate, with more than a faint shake of her head at the pair of them.

'I don't know what these are, this was under a century of muck and feathers.' Bob Guest's hands would need a good wash, too, as he came to the last box of spare kits, looking for a set for Barton Wood.

Jack Higgins could only wait to see what he was given. One attractive silky set in blue had been too small, and another nice set in red and white stripes would be too close to the St Paul's all-red. 'We could always turn out in your Elizabethan costumes!'

Bob Guest finally got the lid off the last box. 'What's this? This looks all right.' He pulled out an amber top, held it up. 'Big enough?'

Jack Higgins took the top, held it to himself. 'They're fair. How many have you got?'

Bob Guest counted. 'Plenty enough.' He tossed around a few black bottoms, too, counted them. 'Don't know when we ever trotted out in these; before my time.' He wiped his hands on one of the tops. 'That's it, then, that's you sorted.'

Jack Higgins was riffling through the box. 'Funny — no 'keeper's jersey.'

'Have one out of here.' Bob Guest took a goal-keeper's top in old-fashioned green from the striped set.

'Gold for glory!' Jack Higgins strapped up the box.

'Glory? Thought this was going to be a friendly, Jack.'

'It had better be, or I'm out of a job!' Jack Higgins lugged the box off the headteacher's side-table. 'It's not the winning or the losing, you know . . .'

'No. Quite right, lad,' the other agreed, with what could have been a wink at his trophies. 'It's the taking part. I know.'

CHAPTER TWELVE

'Wear the colours! Wear the glory colours!'
Mrs Sherry looked at the caretaker, who could take days getting a new tube to a high light, but here he was with an armful of tissue rosettes for giving out to the children who were being walked to the touchline. He'd known the team colours only just before the dinner-break.

'Orange?' Miranda asked, being given a rosette big enough for a parliamentary candidate.

'Amber,' Mr Dunphy told her. 'Blackpool, Wolves, all a bit like this. Colours of glory!'

'Colour of cats' pee!'

A coach hooted in the road. 'Hey up!' Dunphy shouted, at cup-tie pitch already. 'Here come the enemy!'

With long strides, managing not to break into a run, Mrs Sherry was round to the front to meet them before anyone got out of the coach. The full-sized vehicle had stopped, looking large for the road it was in, special, like a cruise ship in a pond. The door hissed open, and out of it came the parent supporters who had travelled with the team – the first a man with a German shepherd dog which got out, sniffed, and barked as if the air were filled with the scent of its prey.

'He'll be all right, love.' The man dragged him to heel. 'Don't like new faces, don't Sabre.'

'Good job mine's old, then. Don't dare let him off that lead!' She waved to where the school field was, and the football pitch, and the waiting Barton Wood children, already skittering about in a litter of tissue. The others followed and walked across the playground in ones and twos, hard eyes on the new school and through its narrow modern windows. A few Barton Wood parents and a couple of older brothers were coming in by the entrance – as well as through the hedge at the back of the field – the first general opening of the grounds, and the feel of a bit of an event.

Mrs Sherry waited at the coach door: because no one else had followed, no team, no teachers. She put her head inside: but as her head went in, Bob Guest came down the aisle from a team talk in the rear seats.

'Bob Guest.' He offered a hand; smart in a new track suit this afternoon, an FA coaching badge stitched upon it.

'Chris Sherry.' She looked behind him. 'Have you got any children in there?'

Bob Guest bent to the window to look out across the field. The Barton Wood team had not run out just yet. 'Keeping them warm. We'll be out directly.'

From inside the school the home team was looking out at the visitors' coach, they were crowded at the windows of Jack Higgins's room: changed as if for PE, but not in their team colours yet.

'Look at the size of that!' Jordan's nose was on the glass.

'You've seen a bus before, Jordan.' Mr Higgins could have been impressed as well, but wasn't letting on. 'Don't get the jitters over a blessed bus!' He rummaged a hand into the box of team strip. 'Come on, stop gawping and put these on.' He started throwing the tops round, to a new sort of nerves now the moment was near.

'Whoa!'

'Hey up!'

'Oooh, Mum!'

'Dead scared to come, Kent!' Lee always had to turn it on to someone else.

Kenny's spaghetti fingers gave up trying to Sellotape his shin-pads round his legs, so he threw them in the bin.

They all looked at one another like at the dress rehearsal of a school play, around at the rest, down at themselves: but even with the amber tops on that magic change somehow hadn't happened: the pictures in their heads had not turned out. With their tops on they'd all thought they'd suddenly look like United, but they didn't: they looked like themselves, a mixed bunch of older and younger kids, bigger and smaller to make up the numbers – and nothing like as impressive as they'd hoped.

'Shorts. Where's the pilkin' shorts?' Matching shorts would soon pull them together.

Mr Higgins started throwing the black bottoms round. 'Come on, get 'em on, we're due out five minutes ago!'

Nicky Power had a loud voice even for whispers – but his shout stopped the room, knees raised, all the one-legged balancers going over. 'Hold up!' He'd been first into the full kit. 'I ain't wearing these!'

They all looked at him, at the complete turn-out. Amber top, and black netball skirt.

Lee was into his. 'Thought they was funny!' He did a Hawaiian dance, wiggle and bum.

'All right for me!' Kompel did a twirl.

'I ain't playing in these! I'm going home 'fore I play in these!' Nicky had his off already.

'Me an' all!' Lee followed. 'They'll see up my legs.'

'Nought to see, is there?'

Sandra tried to look, but Mr Higgins was shouting at them. 'All right, all right! They're netball skirts. Just wear what you had on before!' He looked out of the window at the coach, and said something the children couldn't catch. 'Come on, we've got a football match to play!'

'No – we got a football match to *win*!' Nicky corrected.

To which Mr Higgins made no reply; just nodded.

The team ran out to a straggle of cheers, topped

by a booming Dunphy: 'You Ambers!' It was hard for them not to smile, so some did and some didn't. Lee and Nicky ran with their heads down, kicking up their heels, the way they'd seen it done at Old Trafford: while Sandra came out all arms and legs like a majorette. Kompel and Esi walked, with Esi still the most miserable person on the site, win or lose – everything she did was automatic, going through the motions. Kenny hung back. He'd seen his gran and grandad arriving with Montgomery on a lead.

As they came on to the field and Grandad Bayfield first saw Kenny, Gran put an arm round the old man's waist and they came towards him together.

'You got your guards on?' Grandad wanted to know. It was as if he needed to say something very matter-of-fact.

'I lost 'em. Never mind, eh?'

'No sweat, I made you some spares.' From inside his coat Grandad found another pair, kneeling to the job of putting them down Kenny's socks, while Kenny shut his eyes in the hope Lee Rayner couldn't see. 'And don't forget, turn on a sixpence, use your size, and keep to your position, and when you see the whites of the goalie's eyes, you have a crack – put it high, top right as you're looking. They don't like jumping left, most goalies . . .'

But Kenny wasn't really listening: there was no way he could be paying attention. Having opened his eyes he was staring just like everyone else from

Barton Wood at where the St Paul's team was coming from their coach, no one listening to anyone else any more, even the line gone quiet from its game of floating bits of rosette in the breeze.

Mrs Sherry stared; and Jack Higgins swallowed; and Patrick Dunphy turned round twice and all but fell over. The St Paul's supporters clapped and shouted acclaim, and Sabre their dog barked twice, loud and hard – setting Montgomery off, who wanted at him.

The team was walking from the coach in single file as if this were a Wembley final, led out by the man in the track suit. But it wasn't just the professional way they were walking, as they came on to the pitch and bowed once to each touchline, royal-box stuff; it wasn't the professional way they ran to their end of the pitch and started kicking-in, in their smart up-to-the-mark Manchester United strips. It was their size, and something else. While the Barton Wood team stood there with their mouths open, a self-selected team of everyone fit in the age group, large and small, boys and girls, a right playground pick-up, the St Paul's squad ran tall with oiled legs and Vaselined eyebrows: all Year Six – and all boys. All big boys.

Mrs Sherry looked at Mr Higgins, who smiled like a man who had called for a large round of drinks and forgotten to bring any money.

'They're all boys!' Sandra said.

'You're talking men there!' said Billy Smith.

Kenny was swallowing on nothing.

'Oh, come on! Boys, girls, big, small, that doesn't mean anything ...' But Jack Higgins wouldn't have convinced his two-year-old daughter.

The captain of St Paul's, Miles, a tall boy with a blond tongue of hair down over his forehead, was looking over the opposition. A long, stray ball from the kick-in had brought him down the pitch near to Lee, who had started passing a ball with Nicky so as not to be impressed.

'They've got girls!' Miles called back to a team-mate. 'No one told us we'd be playing girls!'

Lee got to the stray ball first and kicked it off the pitch. 'We ain't all girls, pal!' he told him.

There was a sort of silent growling between the sets of players: and a sudden loud barking from behind the Barton Wood goal where Grandad Bayfield had gone with Montgomery. Sabre was being walked round by his owner and the two dogs had gone for one another in a fighting pyramid in the air: the Barton Wood terrier, and the German shepherd from St Paul's, each held back by the taut length of leather in its owner's hands. Sandra, in goal, had seemed to jump the crossbar in shock.

'Stop it, dogs! Be friendly!'

'That'll be the day! Not trained for it, love,' the St Paul's owner said; while Grandad Bayfield dragged Montgomery away to the far end of the pitch.

In the middle, the two teachers were talking. Jack Higgins was nodding towards his amber squad. 'I've got the team and seven subs. I'll try and give 'em all a run, being a friendly.'

But if he were waiting for some word about St Paul's playing it easy he was disappointed. 'As you like,' Bob Guest told him. 'I'll take first half, you take second.' He blew his Acme Thunderer to summon the captain from each team. Miles trotted into the centre circle, unable to hide a smirk from his headteacher. And while the Barton Wood team stood still, looking at one another, Lee Rayner appointed himself captain, with an eyeball at Miles and a handshake which took his smirk away.

'Come on, you Bartons!'

'Up the Ambers!'

Shrieks of pretend excitement from the line. And, 'Crucify 'em!' from Patrick Dunphy.

'Play football!'

'Play the game!'

'Use your skills, St Paul's!'

From the touchline the differences were clear. St Paul's was lined up in Premier Division style, the patterns they would play clear from the way they were organized, an attacking formation with two up front, five in the midfield, three square across the back, and the keeper patrolling the edge of his penalty box like a border guard. Barton Wood looked as if some strong wind had blown through them. Sandra was alone, way back in goal, jumping about on strings which didn't quite allow her feet ever to touch the ground. Esi and Kompel were waiting for the off but talking about who could have nicked the missing headscarf. Nicky and Lee were up front, but only paired up with each other

– while Jordan, Kenny, Billy Smith and the others were all where they fancied in midfield, all pals in twos, planning glorious passes between each other. And the subs in their topcoats were more interested in catching amber tissue blowing on to the pitch than in the kick-off.

'Spread out, Barton Wood!' Grandad Bayfield shouted. 'Kenny – left! Find yourself space!'

'Work the right!' from Patrick Dunphy. 'They're smaller down the left! A bit.'

'Pass it round!' Jack Higgins shouted to Jordan, the nearest player to him. 'Get it to Nicky and Lee. Always know where Lee is!'

Lee heard him. 'I'll be up there, scoring!' He did a thumbs-up – but the whistle had gone, St Paul's had kicked off, and while Lee was still facing his touchline their forwards had passed him already and were making an early run on the Barton Wood goal. Everyone wearing an amber shirt converged on the player with the ball, who drew them over to his side of the pitch and with a simple lob into the centre found Miles with only Esi to beat, who was just then wondering whether her headscarf could have fallen out of the window and been blown up into a tree. He put the ball through her legs – and there it was, sailing past Sandra, who had come out to flatten a divot.

'Goal!'

'Brilliant!'

'One nil!'

'Offside! Offside, ref !' from Patrick Dunphy.

The St Paul's boys went through a smug routine of touching each other's hands in congratulation as they ran back to their own half of the pitch for the restart.

'Good goal, good goal, Miles,' Bob Guest told his star.

'Never mind! Heads up!' Mrs Sherry shouted. 'Bad luck, Sandra!'

Sandra bowed, as if she'd saved it.

'Spread out, Esi!' Jack Higgins shouted. 'Nicky, back and help. Talk to them, Lee, pick up those runners.'

Lee put his foot on the ball at the centre spot, looked round for the whistle and then passed it to Jordan.

'In hard, now!' Patrick Dunphy shouted. 'Take no prisoners!'

Lee was screaming for the ball to come back to him; but he was being too tightly marked for that – Kenny would have been a better option running outside on the left – and when Jordan did as he was bullied, Lee was robbed and the defender took the ball away up the field and side-footed through to the next line of attack. Kompel threw herself at the player in a brave sliding-tackle, but he'd gone and so had the ball, in a long raking pass like Glen Hoddle of old, and Miles met it with his head to send it hard to Sandra's left as she dived to her right.

Jubilation from St Paul's, all the hand touching again.

'You must watch those runners!' Jack Higgins's voice was already hoarse with the shouting nobody had heard; while Dunphy was going at Nicky Power.

'Get back an' cover, will you? Those girlies don't know nothing! It's open season!'

Which Mrs Sherry had to counter, directly at Bob Guest in the middle. 'Good try, Kompel. Brave tackle! Come on the girls!' She turned to Jack Higgins. 'Did he know we wanted a mixed friendly? They're playing this like the European Cup!'

Jack Higgins stamped his feet on the touchline, philosophic the way losing supporters are. 'Got a feeling he plays everything like the European Cup! Wish we had young David Kent.'

'You're a load of crap, aren't you?' Miles told Lee as they passed each other for the centre kick: simply a matter of fact. He threw the ball at Lee.

'An' you'll be a pile of dust in a minute!'

The whistle blew again, but Lee lost the return to a foul from behind.

'Foul, ref!' Dunphy was shouting. 'Red card! Dirty devil!' Mrs Sherry walked along behind the line for a quiet word in his ear. But there were screams and shouts from the support because Barton Wood had a free kick awarded, the next best thing to a goal.

'Kenny! Up on the edge of the box!' Grandad Bayfield knew where his man ought to be. 'Call for it, boy!'

Jack Higgins ran up the touchline for the first decent chance they'd had. 'Jordan Jenkins take! Lee, Nicky, up on their goal-line. Kompel – edge of the circle.'

Mrs Sherry clapped her hands at Esi. Esi was staring somewhere over the new houses, into the sun. 'Esi! Come on, you're playing football now!' The headteacher shook her head, spotted Sandra, who was trying to calm a mad Montgomery, watching Sabre bark. 'Sandra! Keep your eyes on the game!'

But Lee was doing his own organizing, everyone obeying his pushing and shouting to come up into the goal-mouth. 'Me! Me!' he yelled at Jordan. 'On me head!'

Jordan walked backwards off the ball, counting his paces: a sudden silence while everyone concentrated, except Miranda who slipped away from the line, fed up with watching this rubbish. And rubbish it was. The kick wasn't bad, it had height and power, but with everyone up in the goal-mouth and so far away from him, Jordan felt the need to hit the ball too hard – too much height and too much power – and the goalkeeper caught it out of the air while Lee jumped at nothing. A quick look up showed Miles on his own in the empty half, and with a good half-volley the keeper had it over everyone's heads to the Reds' captain, who gathered, ran on deep and strolled it round Sandra in goal.

The cheer from the St Paul's supporters was still

warm, but it was becoming routine. The advice from the Barton Wood side of the pitch was mixed, and turning to criticism.

'Come on, Ambers! We can do better than this!' And that was Mrs Sherry.

But they couldn't, and within the next minute another goal had been scored, leaving Sandra spread-eagled – from a runner who had rounded Esi just staring down at the grass.

'Sub! Bob!' Jack Higgins was waving from the line. He pointed to Esi and went to push Peter Fielding on. 'Substitute!'

Bob Guest trotted over to him. 'How many have you got?'

'Seven.'

'Bring 'em all on! We'll play the lot. This is doing us no good!'

Mrs Sherry was practically tearing the coats off the substitutes' backs. 'Doing them no good?! Who said this game was for doing them good?'

'No, Bob, keep fair teams,' Jack Higgins was insisting.

'Rubbish!' Mrs Sherry wasn't hearing of it. 'Go out and have a good run!' she told the seven. 'Come on, Barton Wood, let's do us all some good!'

In the centre circle Miles was patting his forelock. 'I'd just as soon have stayed back and done my maths.'

The whistle went, and Lee's centre went hard and straight into Miles's stomach. 'Subtract that, then!' he said. But Miles recovered and, avoiding Lee's wild tackle, took the ball on his own to dribble round Barton Wood and all its subs to score a brilliant goal on his own.

Mr Higgins looked at Mrs Sherry. 'Save us!' he said.

'Could anything?' she asked him coldly.

CHAPTER THIRTEEN

David Kent came running through the school gate, football boots flying. His face was tight with the dried tears of a row with his mother, who'd taken him home and phoned his father – trying for two hours to get him on his mobile – before she'd say whether or not he was coming back to Barton Wood. And by the time the answer was 'yes' she'd left him not wanting to see anyone here ever again – because he knew what he'd get when they saw him. But gut sense told him the football today would be a better return than ordinary school tomorrow; if he wasn't too late. He ran fast across the playground towards the field, rounded a corner – and nearly bowled Mrs Sherry into a litter-bin.

'David!'

'Sorry, Miss.'

She gave him one of her long looks. 'Have you seen Miranda Pudsey?' On some wavelength other than him. 'Not gone through the gate?' He shook his head. 'Then it must be the Nursery!'

'How we doing?'

'Don't ask. Half-time. Just get round there and play!' She went for the Nursery – and David put his head down to get to the field.

The teams had turned round, with Jack Higgins in the middle: and as if impatient for the restart the St Paul's dog Sabre was barking in a rhythm on the far touchline, setting Montgomery off on the near side.

And a howl of delight from Jordan Jenkins. 'David Kent!' he shouted. 'Pos-it-ive!'

'Come on, Dave! Good on you!'

'All right?' Jack Higgins asked Bob Guest – who shrugged, waved an arm: one more player to add to the eighteen wasn't going to make any difference. Patrick Dunphy threw an amber shirt at David, who tangled his fingers all ways in his bootlaces to get on that pitch quick.

The whistle went, and within the first three seconds Miles had won the ball from Lee and laid it off nicely. 'Won't need washing, this shirt!'

'Why?' Lee barged him, off the ball. ''Cos it won't show the blood?'

'Get lost, donkey!'

The two started squaring up, but an Anfield shout from Patrick Dunphy had them spinning instead.

'Yes! That's it! On your own!'

David Kent had got hold of the ball on the right side of midfield, robbing an over-confident Red who'd thought he had all afternoon. Now, attacking the St Paul's goal, Kenny running with him on his left, he played a one-two, controlled the ball again, and ran hard with it towards the penalty area – a strength and a determination about him which took him well past a couple of late tackles from the Reds' defenders. The goalkeeper came quickly off his line to narrow the opportunities, but with a jump over a last wicked leg, David got his toe under the ball and lobbed the man in nets.

'Goal!'

'Great!'

'David Kent! David Kent! David Kent!'

'Yeah!'

It was a good goal. The Barton Wood spectators came back from their boredom games behind the touchline to dance and shout, the St Paul's supporters gave generous applause, and the two dogs barked their heads off at the sudden shouts – pulling at their leads to get to the noise each other was making.

Patrick Dunphy came off the Kop again. 'See?' he yelled at the home side. 'They're tiring! Only another twelve!' He waved a fisted scarf in the air. 'Amber! Amber glory!'

The shouts were heard over in the Nursery, where Mrs Sherry had just found Miranda.

'Have you made me miss our only goal?'

Miranda hunched her shoulders. She hadn't been playing, hadn't wanted to play, and she didn't give a toss. She definitely hadn't wanted to stand watching, she was better off teaching painting in here.

She turned back to the child she was showing. 'See, in the colour, on the sponge, mix, and on the paper. Easy, innit? And it don't run down the easel then.' She was demonstrating in red, guiding a little girl's hand. 'She's got it now,' she told Mrs Sherry.

'Good. Now come on, I want to see what's going on out there . . .'

But even as she led Miranda by the hand, it was something else in the room that took her attention. A Nursery child in a long tripping-up dress and high-heeled shoes, heading for the Home Corner and carrying a black doll in her arms, which was dressed up special, too, wrapped in a pretty piece of material. 'I'm gonna get married,' the child said, 'an' my little baby's gonna be my bridesmaid.'

'Lovely,' said Mrs Sherry. 'And what a pretty pattern on her gown . . . Where did your bridesmaid get this?'

'I give it her,' Miranda said, matter-of-fact. 'Nice, innit?'

A loud whistle from outside turned Mrs Sherry's head again. She hurried to the window as she unwound the bridesmaid's gown from the doll. Jack Higgins was running to the centre circle where Miles was lying on the ground.

'Oh no!' she said. 'An incident!'

Out on the field Mr Higgins was giving Lee the straight arm and the long point: 'Off! Off, Lee Rayner!'

Lee, not upset by the decision, just smiled at Miles who was sitting up, crying, his shirt quite dirty now.

On the line Patrick Dunphy threw a coat round Lee. 'Come on now, the eighteen men!' he yelled.

On the pitch David Kent was starting to reorganize the team. He sent Jordan and Kompel back into position, stood sad Esi back in the centre of the last line of defence, got Kenny to drop back alongside him. 'Now, keep your shape. Face the ball . . .' And Barton Wood stood ready for the free kick. But ready or not, transformed or not by a real captain, time was running out. As the game restarted Jordan was asking Jack Higgins how long there was to go.

'Six minutes.'

Right from the off a battle was going on for the ball between David Kent and two Reds: with Miles on his feet again and deciding to get involved.

'We can't win in six minutes!'

David Kent sent Kenny away down the left, who, with support on his right, was able to use his size to nip round a slow-turning back and lay the ball off to Jordan. Sandra, now on the pitch and Billy Smith in goal, ran into Mr Higgins, who was keeping up with play. He just stopped himself from swallowing his whistle and gave a throw-in to Reds.

'How long till the end?' Sandra wanted to know.

'Not long enough.'

'Then that's not fair!' Now Sandra was running round with him, sewn on like Peter Pan's shadow. 'They cheated us! They knew we was only a little school and they came here like United. They're pathetic, rotten sports! Aren't they?' She stood in his way, made him pull up like a boy racer at the lights. 'You never wanted us to have this!'

Jack Higgins looked at the girl: the school clown, soppy Sandra who got everything wrong: except she was right, here. This hadn't been what was expected: Bob Guest had come along to humiliate them, to show his parents what a class school his was compared to this new outfit – and no doubt hoping Councillor Bamber might be here to underline it.

'Wish there'd be an earthquake.'

'Don't be silly, Sandra.'

The trouble was, everyone knew it *was* all a bit late. The game was a lot more even with David Kent bringing some sense to the side, thinking for the team instead of just the glory of his own goals, but time was running out too fast. Even with the new support from the line, Mrs Sherry waving a headscarf in the air and shouting louder than Dunphy now, there wouldn't be the time to pull the match back. As the tackles went in and passes went astray and children ran themselves breathless for the ball, the result of the match was in no doubt.

'Come on you St Paul's!' And Sabre barked like a canon.

'You Ambers!'

'What if there *is* an earthquake?' Sandra was still under Jack Higgins's feet.

'Match abandoned, I suppose.' He whistled for another throw.

'Who wins when it's 'bandoned?'

Jack Higgins looked at his watch, saw David Kent going off on another run and ran following himself. 'No one. Not if . . . it doesn't go to . . . full time.' He was out of breath, out of condition.

David had got into the penalty area but he couldn't quite place the final pass well enough for Kenny, who'd made a good run to get on to it. There was a clap from all sides, and cheers from Dunphy and Grandad Bayfield – which set Sabre and Montgomery off again, each at the other as if they were playing the match between them.

'Goal-kick.' Jack Higgins turned to run back up-field, did a little hop so as not to bump into his shadow. But she wasn't there. He whistled, and the ball came looping over his head – him running backwards as he looked again at his watch – to be tripped by a dog suddenly taking the direct route across the pitch.

'Monty! Come here!' Grandad Bayfield was running on after, the dog's lead loose in his hand. 'Who let him off?'

Montgomery ran yapping at Sabre who, with a tug which would have shifted Samson, wrenched away from his master and answered the challenge with barks and bites and backward-leaping yelps. And all at once there was no playing on with the canine battle and the pitch invasion which followed. Sandra, pleased with her secret unleashing, trotted back as the nearer players ran to the dogs going for it in the middle of the centre circle; the brave little

Montgomery turning on a sixpence and frustrating the tail-chasing Sabre, with children grabbing at Sabre's lead but frightened to the spine by the sudden turning and barking; pushed aside by parents and staff who weren't wanting to see children getting injured.

But no one could part the dogs. It was all bark, bite, yelp, dodge, roll, scrabble, snarl – hair and spit flying, Montgomery running round and darting in, the top dog, with Sabre slow, angry, chasing anything, white slices of mouth and hard eyes.

'Come here!'

'Get back!'

'Down, boy!'

'Stay!'

'Get off !'

'Help!'

At last, Grandad Bayfield got in and solved it. He pulled Kenny's shin-guards from out of the boy's stockings and threw them into Sabre's path for mauling, which gave the grabbing hands of his owner that one chance to catch hold of his lead.

'Here, boy, heel! Stay! Stay for Daddy!'

Bob Guest was running over to Jack Higgins, looking at his watch. And Patrick Dunphy was running over, too: got there as the teachers stood facing one another.

'I think one of our kids got bit,' the caretaker interrupted.

Jack Higgins looked at the man. 'Very badly, Mr Dunphy?' he asked.

'One of the young ones. He could have been, or he need not have been, it's hard to tell with the red stuff running.' He put his hand on Bob Guest's arm. 'But he's a good sport, this man – he wouldn't want us to soldier on with seventeen men.'

That seemed to make up Jack Higgins's mind. He blew his whistle. 'Match abandoned!' he announced.

'Abandoned?' Bob Guest almost reached for a rule-book.

'Dogs stopped play. Injured player. Couldn't play to full time. Shame. Result – null and void!'

'Match 'bandoned!' Sandra shouted.

There were moans, and there were cheers: there were sulks and there were smiles: and there was a Barton Wood coming together in the middle, hugs and thumps on the back, and reruns of their glory moments.

Except for Esi – who couldn't have cared less what the result was; there was only one result she would ever have wanted today. Things went well for some, and they went badly for others. Looking at the Barton Wood faces around her she could see the up they were on: they hadn't actually lost to St Paul's and they were on the biggest high since the school had opened. While for her . . .

She looked across at Mrs Sherry who was waving children away from any arguing with the St Paul's people. Waving them away with something she had flapping in her hand.

With a headscarf. *Her* headscarf! 'Miss! Miss!'

Her feet kept fleeting touch with the ground as she got over to the headteacher; as near to flying as there is. 'Miss! Where was it?'

Mrs Sherry smiled, handed it over. 'In the Nursery, looking beautiful on an African bridesmaid.'

'Ah!' Esi clutched it to her, couldn't see out for the tears, couldn't speak for the swallow. 'Ah!'

'Pos–it–ive!' said Jordan, coming up.

Esi looked at him, held the headscarf on, smiled. 'Pos–it–ive?' she asked, looking like the bridesmaid of all the world.

'Yeah – we drew! We drew! We drew!' He ran to find Kenny, to jump on his back.

But while Esi could fly, nothing could knock Kenny over, either. His gran and his grandad were coming towards him, Montgomery still jumping as if he were on elastic, all in winning moods.

'Well done, pal. You done well when you started playing. There's a few proud of you today, I'll tell you!' The old man sniffed, and turned away to look at the empty goal.

Yeah, Kenny thought; them, and his dad at work. And, who knew . . .? He looked to his feet. He was standing where he'd lain that day a week or so back, looking at this school with fear and dread, that day he'd been frozen out of the football and threatened over the casey, when it had all looked so bad. Now he was standing here covered in mud and feeling proud. He rubbed his nose. He hadn't done marvels on the pitch, but he'd done well enough, he'd turned on a sixpence a couple of times, pleased his grandad, put in a few good passes and nearly got on to a goal. He looked around, savouring the moment. And Jordan was there . . . and Lee, who was going to some of the Barton Woods giving out a hug. He came Kenny's way: on his way past to Nicky?

'They nearly won the game, Ken – but we won the fights!' And he hugged Kenny, too: probably the best hug for Kenny ever since the last one he'd had off his mother. He hugged him back: because *Ken*, he'd said – not *Titch* or *Midget* or *Shorty*: Lee Rayner had called him *Ken*. He looked at his grandad, and he just managed not to wink.

The St Paul's boys had already got back to their coach, which was pulling away without hooting, leaving the Barton Wood people nothing to do but walk back into the school like a straggle of refugees claiming new ground; but with their heads held very high: and all uncovered to the pale Lancashire sun except for one, which was wearing a beautiful headscarf.